Lone Wolves

Books by John Smelcer

Fiction

The Trap
The Great Death
Edge of Nowhere
Alaskan: Stories from the Great Land

Native Studies

The Indian Prophet
The Raven and the Totem
A Cycle of Myths
In the Shadows of Mountains
What Raven Said
The Day That Cries Forever
Durable Breath
Native American Classics

Poetry

Songs from an Outcast
Riversong
Without Reservation
Beautiful Words
Tracks
Raven Speaks

Lone Wolves

John Smelcer

Leapfrog Press
Fredonia, New York

Published in 2013 in the United States by
Leapfrog Press LLC
PO Box 505
Fredonia, NY 14063
www.leapfrogpress.com

Printed in the United States of America

Distributed in the United States by
Consortium Book Sales and Distribution
St. Paul, Minnesota 55114
www.cbsd.com

First Edition

ISBN: 978-1-935248-55-2

Library of Congress Cataloging-in-Publication Data

Information available at the Library of Congress

3 1461 00289 3425

for my daughters, Zara and Ayiana,
born almost a quarter century apart

Acknowledgements

The author would like to thank Bard Young, Rod Clark and Melanie Werth, Susan Romanczuk, Lisa and Michael Graziano, and Lindsey Buck for their editorial suggestions. He would also like to thank Ann Weinstock for her striking cover design and Hannah Carlon for her inside illustration. He especially appreciates David Collins for being a critical sounding board during the original concept stage, as well as Ray Bradbury for his kind words on the cover and Alexandra Bradbury for renewing the estate's permission to use them.

A Note for Readers

A glossary of Alaska Native words and dog sledding terms used throughout this story appears at the end of the book. All Indian words come from the author's *Ahtna Noun Dictionary and Pronunciation Guide* (1998, 2011; foreword by Noam Chomsky and Steven Pinker), which was originally published by The Ahtna Heritage Foundation. To learn more about the author go to www.johnsmelcer.com

Contents

After making the world and the sun, moon, and stars; after making all the seas, lakes, and rivers; after making all the birds, animals, and fish, Raven found the first people cowering inside a clamshell. Seeing they were frightened of the world, Raven taught the people how to hunt and fish and how to make shelter and fire. Most importantly, she taught them language. Raven told the people to give names to everything she had created, even the stars. For a long time, people gave names to all living things, big and small, as well as to rivers, creeks, lakes, hills, glaciers, and mountains. Everything had a name. And for a long time, those things knew the names they had been given. Bear, Wolf, and Wolverine knew their names. Rabbit, Squirrel, and Fox knew their names. Back then, mountains always returned their names when they were called upon. It was as if the earth and the people were the same. But after a very long time, humanity fashioned new gods with new languages, and the people began to forget the language that Raven had given them, and the animals and mountains no longer remembered their names, and the earth and the people were no longer the same.

1

Łts'ii c'eliis
Song of the Wind

In a wide valley—far away from bustling boulevards and traffic jams, street lights and parking meters, far away from sidewalks and crosswalks, far away from shopping malls and fast food chains—a frozen river winds through snow-covered foothills. In the boundless distance beyond the floodplain, the jagged peaks of mountains jut into a blue and cloudless sky. And on the frozen river, eight dogs pull a wooden sled over the rattling ice. The driver stands on a small platform at the back holding on with both hands, peering through the wolf-trimmed hood of a parka, mindful of the trail ahead, and ready at any moment to command the dog at the front of the line with a single word. A yellow snowmobile follows behind. Ahead, the packed trail steers away from a perilous stretch of open water. As they edge dangerously close, vapor rises from the river and billows from the labored breathing of the dogs. Both sled and machine veer off the river and turn up a steep bank, which leads into the forest. At the crest, the sled tips and throws the driver, who scrambles to chase the runaway sled until it vanishes around a bend in the trail. The yellow snowmobile pulls alongside briefly, and the sledless musher climbs aboard. For almost a mile, the two follow the sled until, finally, they are able to cut it off and stop the oblivious dogs. The thrown musher dashes to the back of the sled and steps on the foot brake.

"Set the hook, Denny!" shouted the old man sitting on the idling snowmobile.

The sled driver reached for the metal claw attached to a short rope, and with one hand still gripping the sled, set the hook onto the packed trail and stomped on it, driving the long, curved teeth deep to anchor the sled, and then tied the snub line to a tree, the way one ties off a boat to keep it from drifting away downriver.

At first the yelping dogs strained to move the sled, but then settled, realizing they weren't going anywhere.

"You still have a lot to learn," said the old man, pressing the kill-switch on the handlebars to shut off the noisy engine. "Let's rest and have lunch here."

The sled driver pulled back the fur-trimmed hood, revealing long, black hair and the smiling face of a 16-year-old girl!

"Sounds good to me, Grandpa."

The grandfather dug out a hatchet from a large bag nestled in the sled's basket.

"You go cut firewood while I get the dogs off the line."

The old man shuffled to the front of the team, snow crunching beneath his boots.

"Line out!" he said sternly to the lead dog, named Kilana, who was staring keenly at the man, his head cocked, waiting for any signal.

The white-and-yellow husky understood the command. Immediately, he tugged against the anchored sled, pulling the other dogs forward, drawing the tow line taut. Without speaking, the old man deftly unhooked the dogs from the line and tied each one to a tree far enough from others to avoid fights over food. At times, when trees were unavailable—which was often the case—he used metal stakes or a long tether line. While he worked, his granddaughter collected wood for a fire, carrying several armfuls, which she piled in a heap on the side of the trail.

Within minutes, all eight dogs were unharnessed from the sled, and a large pot of water was heating over a crackling fire. When the water was warm, but not too hot, each dog received a scoop of dry food with a chunk of dried salmon and a cup of the warm water poured into a metal dish. The salmon were caught in the summer and fall and hung and dried and stored to feed the dogs all winter long. While the lithe dogs ate greedily, as if starving, licking the bowls clean, the girl and her grandfather shared their lunch of dried salmon strips, biscuits, and homemade blueberry jam.

A pot of coffee was percolating on the fire, the little glass bulb atop the blackened pot filling with brown liquid every few seconds as if measuring time.

Camp time.

"I love it out here," said the old man, smiling as he looked at the frozen river, the lonely sled, and the mountains in the distance. "This is home."

The girl nodded.

Neither said a word as they stood by the fire, listening to the wind singing in the trees and the caw of a raven far off. The dogs rested, quiet and content with full bellies. Some pulled ice from between their toes with their teeth. Two were curled up fast asleep, their bushy tails covering their face.

Deneena, for that was Denny's given name, broke the silence.

"Grandfather, teach me some more words."

The old man, whose name was Sampson, crouched to pour a cup of coffee and then stood, cupping both hands around the warm cup.

"Let's see," he said, looking around him. "I've taught you so many already. Let me test you. What is the word for tree?" he asked, pointing at a nearby spruce tree.

"That's easy. *Ts'abaeli*. Come on, Grandpa. Give me something harder."

The old man pointed at the far mountains.

"What is the word for mountains?"

"*Ghelaay*," boasted the girl. "That was easy, too."

"Okay. But what do you call *that* particular one?" he asked, pointing to the tallest mountain on the horizon.

Deneena was temporarily stumped. She searched her memory, struggling to remember when she had heard the name.

"K . . . Kell . . ." I know it starts with a K," she grumbled, angry with herself for not remembering.

"*K'ełt'aeni*," replied Sampson with a smile. "For thousands of years, Indians been calling that mountain *K'ełt'aeni*. But first White man comes along, sees that mountain, writes down some English name on a map, and people call it that ever since. Same thing goes for almost everything. No one remembers Indian names. It so bad, I think dogs even bark in English nowadays."

Denny laughed at her grandfather's joke.

She loved the word game, which they played often. But to the old man it was no game at all. Very few people spoke their language any longer, only the very old, like himself. His wife and maybe a dozen others still spoke it. But none of their children, including Denny's mother, had ever learned it. It was important to the old man that some of the younger generation try to keep the language alive, at least a little while longer. Denny was the only grandchild who had showed any interest at all. She liked to learn the words from her grandparents and from other elders, writing them down in her own little dictionary. She also wrote down the old stories they told her, the ones about Raven. Without even realizing it, Denny was a kind of anthropologist-in-training, a documenter of culture. He was proud of her for that and for the way she wanted to learn other old things, like their customs and traditions, such as mushing a dogsled and catching and drying salmon on a fish rack, smoking them slowly with green, leafy alder branches tossed on a smoldering fire, until the meat glazed over hard enough so that flies couldn't lay their eggs and ruin the meat.

Just then a curious raven flew overhead.

"*Saghani*," proclaimed the girl, looking at her grandfather for approval.

"Very good."

With a slight breeze blowing campfire smoke into his face, making him squint, the old man poured another cup of coffee. Then he stood away from the smoke.

"Our people been living on this land for thousands of years, Denny. It's part of us. That river's been sliding past our village ever since flowing water carved its bed. Them mountains been looking down on us for even longer. Our world goes from here to there and from there to there," he said pointing at mountains all around them, some very far away.

The girl turned her head to follow his finger, her blues eyes taking in everything.

"We are part of the land," he continued, "and the land is part of us. We give it names and the names become part of us. We see the world in a particular way—*our* way—because of the words we give it. This is *my* world. This is *your* world. It takes care of us, provides for us; and we must take care of it."

"I feel the same way, Grandpa," replied Deneena, with a reverence in her voice.

The old man smiled broadly.

"I know you do," he said, putting a hand on the girl's shoulder. "That why I bring you out here."

When the break was over, the two worked together to hook the dogs back up to the tow line, careful not to entangle them. Sometimes they had to lift a dog and place him on the correct side of the line. The dogs already connected were anxious to go, straining against the steadfast snub line and whining. Sled dogs love to run. They were born for it. They dream of it all summer long. When the musher first brings out the sled, they jump and bark, happy knowing that they will soon be on the trail.

Once every dog was hooked up properly, Sampson untied the snub line and set it in the basket. When they were both ready, the old man pressed the ignition button and started his snowmobile, waving her to go. Denny pulled the snow hook and stood on the platform at the back of the sled runners, gripping the handle tightly.

"Go!" she shouted.

With a sharp yank the excited dogs burst down the trail, while Denny pedaled at first, pushing with one foot to help get the sled started, as a skateboarder would.

"Gee!" she shouted again moments later when they came to the frozen river.

From years of training, Kilana turned right. He understood the difference between *gee* and *haw*: right and left. A good lead dog has to know many words.

And he has to be fast.

The swing dogs, those immediately behind the lead, helped to turn the rest of the team.

Several miles down the trail, a herd of caribou were milling about on the frozen river. When the caribou saw the sled and snowmobile approaching, they jogged off the river and into the trees.

Eighteen miles downriver, the sled pulled off into the village. The snowmobile followed. When they arrived at their small cabin, the old man helped to unhook the dogs and tie each one to his little, flat-roofed dog house filled with a pile of straw for bedding. When all the dogs were off the line, Deneena carefully put away the rigging, as she had been taught. She put blocks of wood under the sled runners to keep them from freezing solid to the ground or from building up with ice. When all the work was done, the two walked into the warm house, first stomping their boots on a large mat outside.

A delicious aroma greeted them.

"What's cooking, Grandma?" asked Denny while hanging her parka on a nail beside the door.

"None of your business. That's what's cooking," replied the old woman with a grin.

"Come on, Grandma. What is it?"

I'll give you a hint—*udzih taas,*" she answered in Indian.

"Caribou soup! I knew it."

After removing her boots, Denny examined the large pot simmering on the stove. The end of a long bone was sticking out. She leaned over and waved the fumes toward her nose with a hand.

"It smells good."

"It'll warm your insides," said her grandmother.

Denny's mother entered the small cooking area.

"Out of my kitchen you two. Out, out," she said, shooing them away with her hands.

She lifted the bone out of the pot, set it on a board, and sliced the tender meat from it, cutting it into bite-size chunks. When she was done, she lifted the board and used the knife to slide the meat back into the pot.

"Soup's on!" she yelled to everyone.

The family of four sat at the small plywood table, eating their supper and talking.

"How was the trail?" asked Denny's mother.

"It was pretty fast, Delia," said her father. "That last snow gave it a good base. A couple more inches be really good."

"And how did my daughter do today?"

"She did fine. She gonna be a great musher, like I was long time ago."

The mother looked at her daughter across the table.

"Why you always out in the woods with them dogs?" she said,

shaking her head in disapproval. "That's no place for a girl your age. Why don't you spend more time with other kids from school doing normal things? What am I going to do with you?"

Denny shrugged her shoulders and said nothing, looking down at the table, fumbling with her spoon. She had heard her mother say the same thing a hundred times.

Instead, Sampson answered.

"It's okay, Delia. She still young . . . just trying to figure out who she is and who she's going to be. It don't hurt nothing."

"Stay out of it, Dad," snapped Delia. "She's *my* daughter. She's a teenage girl for Chrissake. She shouldn't be out in the woods all day running a dogsled. And what about *you*?" she demanded. "You shouldn't be out there, neither. What if you have another heart attack? Do you ever think about that?"

Sampson didn't reply. He, too, had learned it was better to say nothing. He picked up his empty bowl and handed it to his wife.

"*Taas utanittl'iit, ts'inst'e'e,*" he said, in a tone that sounded like an order.

Denny understood that he was asking for more soup.

Her grandmother filled the bowl and handed it back.

"*Gah, da'atnae,*" she grumbled. "Here, Old Man."

The grandparents smiled at each other. It was a game they played. Truth be told, they were very happy together. They had been married for fifty-one years. At forty, Delia was the youngest of their five children. The oldest was almost fifty.

When supper was finished, Delia turned to her daughter.

"Tomorrow's Monday. Did you finish all your homework?"

"I need to finish a paper for history," replied Denny, setting her empty bowl in the sink.

"Get working on it and then take a bath before bed," said Delia in a motherly fashion.

Denny marched over and plopped onto a chair beside the wood stove. It was the warmest place in the house. For almost an hour she read from a book and wrote in a notebook. While she worked, a large pot of water was heating on the stove. When the water was warm, Denny carried the pot behind a curtain in the back of the cabin and set it down beside a large, galvanized wash tub, just large enough for a person to kneel or crouch in. She took off her clothes and stepped into the tub. Using a tin cup, she poured warm water over her head, washed her long hair and body, and then used the rest of the water to rinse. With no plumbing, the house had no bathtub or toilet. Water was hauled from the river in five-gallon buckets, each weighing forty pounds. In winter, they kept open a hole in the ice, covering it with a Styrofoam board and snow to keep it from freezing over.

Everyone used an outhouse, called *tsa hwnax* in Indian, a dozen yards or so behind the cabin, even when it was 60 degrees below zero. At such extreme temperatures, solid waste froze almost immediately, each successive go landing atop the last and freezing solid until—after months of winter use—from the bottom of the outhouse hole arose a brown, frozen stalagmite reaching upward almost to the seat-hole, posing risk of impalement to any unwary user. In early summer, it would finally melt, tumble over like a stack of blocks, and ooze into a putrid, brown, semi-liquid. Scoops of lye would help it dissolve further.

Also behind the cabin was a small sweathouse, called *sezel*, which the family used regularly to take steam baths. In their language, the words for Saturday and Sunday were related to use of the sweathouse. Denny loved to sit in the sauna, sweat dripping off her body, while reading a book by candlelight, stepping out every so often to cool down.

The cabin itself consisted of one large room with the small kitchen, the dining table, and a small sitting area facing the wood stove. A narrow bed was pushed against a wall for Denny. An addition had been built at the back of the house, which was one large room with a rickety wall separating the area where Denny's mother and grandparents slept. All in all, it was a cozy home, especially when the temperature outside plummeted.

Once in bed, Denny took out her diary, which she hid behind a row of books on a single shelf beside her small bed. She thumbed through it until she found the first blank page. Then she began to write:

Mother doesn't understand me at all. How can we be so different? Why does she want me to be someone I'm not? What's wrong with the way I am? Other girls in the village drink all the time and get pregnant before they even graduate high school, like Mary Paniaq. Almost everybody at school drinks and smokes pot. She should be glad I don't do any of that stuff. Today, Grandpa talked about how the land is his home. He loves it out there. I thought I'd write a poem about him. I'm afraid it's not a very good one. I think I spelled the Indian words right.

Home

Standing on a frozen bank of the river,
snowy mountains in the distance.

Waiting for the river to replace his blood.
Waiting for the earth to replace his bones.

Ghak'ae

*Yihwnighi'aa sdaghaay dlii 'Atna',
ghelaay nadaexi zaadi.*

*De baa 'Atna' tuu naat'aan del.
De baa nen' naat'aan ts'en.*

2

Nen' tae dlii
Land of Ice

When Denny stepped out the front door early the next morning on her way to school, the dogs began barking and jumping. Some howled from atop their little houses.

"Settle down," she said in a stern voice. "Grandpa will feed you soon."

One by one, the raucous dogs quieted.

As she passed other small houses along the way, dogs tied up in front yards barked and growled at her. There were more dogs in the village than people.

The main road through the village ran alongside the wide river. Denny passed a small wooden cross about waist high adorned with plastic flowers, their bright colors faded from years of sunlight.

It was a reminder of the life and death of Maggie Yazzie.

Maggie was Denny's cousin, and although Maggie was several years older, they had grown up together. Each was the closest the other had to a sister. All through junior high and high school, Maggie had earned straight As. Everyone in the village bragged about how smart she was. Maggie wanted to earn a degree in nursing and come back to the village to help her people. On the day that she flew off to go to college in the big city, the whole community turned out at the little airstrip to see her off and to wave goodbye.

Once at the college, though, Maggie was tested so that she could be placed in the right classes. Even though she had taken senior-level English and math and science, one test showed that she could barely read at an eighth or ninth grade level, while another showed that her command of math was that of a seventh or eighth grader. She was told that she would have to take a year of remedial classes just to prepare her for the required college-level courses. Because of her low scores, she was not accepted into the highly competitive nursing program.

The news really hurt Maggie. But it was more than wounded pride; it was a melting of dreams. Denny remembered a conversation they had when Maggie came home for Christmas.

"I think teachers lie to us," Maggie said, as they walked through the village, snow crunching beneath their boots.

Denny could tell that Maggie's despair was as suffocating as a packed snowdrift.

"What do you mean?"

Maggie didn't reply at first, as if she was thinking, choosing her words carefully.

"I think some teachers believe that Native children will never grow up to be anything or do anything important, so they give us good grades to make us feel good about ourselves, to make the community feel good."

"That's not right," said Denny, wondering about her own good grades. "That can't be right. We have plans and futures just like all them kids in the cities."

Maggie nodded and frowned.

"They think that because there's so much alcoholism and depression and suicide that they have to lie to us," said Maggie. "But you can't prepare a person for the future by lying. It's not right."

For the rest of the walk, the two girls talked about how ill-prepared they all were for the world beyond their village. Denny was saddened by her cousin's sadness, but she felt strengthened by their talking. She felt like a little sister learning from a big sister.

Then Maggie said something Denny didn't expect.

"Nothing matters anymore," she half-whispered in a voice as sad and stripped of life as a bear-killed moose carcass partially buried in the earth.

Denny didn't know what to say at the time, but in the following years, she replayed that moment a thousand times in her mind, offering the consoling words she never said.

Maggie returned to college after the vacation and spent the semester taking more remedial classes. She struggled, not only with school, but also with her loneliness and disappointment, until one day she returned to the village during spring break-up, when the frozen river shakes itself loose of the banks and begins to flow again, jumbled sheets of ice and icebergs grinding their way to the sea.

Birdie Kawagley, who lived in the small log cabin on the other side of the dirt road, said she saw Maggie standing on the riverbank for a long time, just watching the flowing ice and listening to the grinding river. She said she paid no mind at first. But then she saw Maggie jump onto a passing sheet of ice and stand in the middle as the river carried her downriver.

"She just stood there, as calm as can be," Birdie told the state trooper who flew into the village to investigate her death.

Maggie's body was never found.

That account was not as unusual as one might think. Denny knew that Alaska Natives, especially young men, committed suicide at a rate a dozen times higher than that of the rest of America. One out of five young men kills himself by the age of twenty-five. Village cemeteries were full of the corpses of failed and dead dreams. Denny had even heard of a 12-year-old boy in a village up north who simply walked off across the frozen arctic tundra at 60 below zero, into the teeth of the wind.

Denny stopped for a minute and stared at the cross.

"I'm sorry," she said aloud.

She wiped a tear from her cheek, hard, almost with anger, and then walked away.

The sun-dulled flowers waved in the slight wind.

Denny's school was like any other school in the bush. It was the most modern building in the village, with a furnace, running water and toilets, telephones, a fax machine, and the Internet. It even had a gymnasium, which was often used for community functions. In many ways, the school was the heart of any village. In the old days, village children were often relocated to larger communities to attend school from fall to spring. But for a generation, schools had been built in almost every village that had children. More recently, however, for reasons largely economic, an exodus had drained the villages of families, which move to the larger cities where traditions and cultural values and languages gave way to modernity, to malls and cineplexes, to megastores with endless parking lots, to coffeehouses and bistros, and to boulevards lined with fast-food and convenience stores. In the unfamiliar and unfriendly environment, children from small villages were intimidated or lost in the sea of hundreds, even thousands, of students at the city schools.

Denny's school had only a few classrooms and only a few teachers, who had to be qualified to teach a number of subjects and to serve in various administrative capacities. In the entire school, there were only nine high-school-aged students, Denny among them. Several grades were lumped together, the teachers doing the best they could in such an environment, where students might be two or three grades apart from one another. Denny often wondered about the challenges of teaching math or reading to such groups, the culture-shock to a teacher unfamiliar with village life.

When she was in seventh grade, Denny accidentally overheard a conversation between two teachers after school.

"I can't take anymore," said the new teacher from California. "I didn't sign up for this."

"But you have a contract," replied the other, seasoned teacher.

"I don't care. I wasn't prepared to live like this. No one can. I'm going home."

Within a week that teacher was flying south like a goose in the fall.

During second period, while the teacher was busy writing on the board, a note was passed around class. When it reached Deneena, she unfolded it beneath the desktop to read.

"Party at Mary's house tonight. Parents out of town. BYOB! Pass it on."

Mary's parents were always gone, leaving their 16-year-old daughter to fend for herself. The few occasions they were home, they were always drunk and abusive.

Deneena quietly folded the note, and, when the teacher was looking away, she tossed it to Johnny Shaginoff. At lunch, almost all of the high school students huddled behind the school where no one would see them. Half of them wore no jacket, even though the temperature was around zero. Johnny, a junior, lit a joint, took a hit, and passed it to his left. Each student took a hit, including Mary Paniaq, who was beginning to show beneath her parka. Most people in the village just thought she was putting on some weight, which was common during the long, dark, boring months.

When the joint came to Denny, she passed it directly to Silas Charley, without taking a puff. Silas held it to his pursed lips for a moment before passing it to the next person. Silas was the same age as Denny. He rarely spoke, even in class. When teachers called on him during class, they'd chastise him for mumbling at the floor when he spoke. Denny liked Silas, but she didn't like that he drank and did drugs like everyone else.

"Hey, Denny," said Johnny, "how come you never do nothin' fun? Why you always such a stick in the mud?"

"Yeah," agreed Norman Fury, a senior who was the school's best basketball player. "It's probably because she ain't got no father."

"I don't know," replied a hurt Denny, not looking anyone in the eye. She hated when people reminded her that her father didn't want anything to do with her. "I just don't want to, I guess."

"You never wanna do anything," said Mary. "Maybe you have some of *this* instead," she added, pulling out a small silver flask from inside her parka.

"What's in it, Mary?" asked Johnny.

"My friend Jim . . . Beam."

Everyone laughed and took short sips from the flask, except for Denny, who passed it the way she had passed the joint.

Just then a squirrel climbed out to the end of a spruce bough and chattered at the group. Johnny made a snowball and threw it at the squirrel, missing it, but the frightened animal fled nonetheless, jumping from bough to bough until it was safely several trees away.

"Hey, Denny," said Johnny. "What's the Indian word for squirrel?"

"*Dligi*," she replied, proudly.

Johnny repeated the word.

"What a stupid word," he said. "Why you waste your time with that old-fashioned crap?"

"Yeah," agreed Norman. "That stuff is lame. I can't wait to get outta this stupid village and move to a city."

"I don't know. Just seems important somehow," said Denny as she watched Mary take a swig from the flask. "You know that's bad for the baby?"

"Hell, *everything's* bad for this baby. Life's gonna be bad for it.

Might as well start gettin' use to it now." Mary gave a little snicker before taking another swig.

And there was a kind of sad truth in her words. Only Deneena and the other students standing in the cold behind the school knew what had happened to Mary. She had told them in confidence. Her own cousin, Willy Paniaq, seven years older, had raped her when they were both drunk and got her pregnant. In small, remote villages, where there were few unrelated girls or women, men often raped their own relatives. And no one did anything about it. The victims had no recourse, no one to talk to. Their own mothers, many having endured the same thing, warned them not to tell anyone.

"That's your cousin," mothers scolded their daughters. "What's wrong with you? You want your cousin to go to jail?"

Whether from shame or from a strong sense of community or from something else, something deep and hard and as frozen as a dead animal, villages protected the rapist, not the victim. The way her stomach was growing, Mary wouldn't be able to hide her secret for much longer. Everyone in the village would know soon enough.

'Hell, it's time to go back in," said Norman, looking at his watch. "Damn, it's cold out here!"

As they shuffled around the building, Denny stopped for a moment and marveled at the wide, frozen river, beckoning to her, a friendly highway leading into the mountains. Silas Charley stopped and waited for her, rubbing his hands together to warm them.

"I think the word for squirrel is pretty cool," he said, in his quiet way.

Less than an hour later, during math, Ms. Stevens, who taught English and history, staggered into the classroom and stood in the doorway, her eyes red and swollen from crying, a wad of tissue clutched in one hand.

"I . . . I have some bad news," she half whispered.

The nine students stopped what they were doing.

"Elie Holbert died yesterday."

Everyone gasped. Ms. Holbert taught English and social studies at the village thirty miles upriver. The two small schools often partnered on projects and sports, especially basketball and volleyball. Everyone liked her.

"What happened?" two students asked at the same time.

"She was . . ." Ms. Stevens tried to choke back her emotions. She had been close friends with Elie, who was about her age. "She was out jogging alone when a pack of wolves attacked her about two miles from the village."

Denny put a hand to her mouth.

Several students burst into tears.

Everyone knew that Ms. Holbert was a runner. She was barely five feet tall and as skinny as an icicle. She had an endearing Southern accent that was strange to hear in a village so far north.

"They say the wolves were still on her when someone came along on a snowmobile and frightened them away. I just got a phone call from the school."

No one wanted to believe the news. Elie Holbert was a good person. But everyone in the grieving classroom knew that wolves could be dangerous, contrary to the popular opinion by city folks who have never seen one in the wild. An empty belly on a vast and frozen land can be a dangerous thing.

Denny stood up and hugged Ms. Stevens, her favorite teacher, who always challenged students to think for themselves. Mary joined the embrace while the rest looked down at the floor or out the window, trying to hide their grief.

When school was over, Denny practically ran home. As usual, the dogs barked excitedly when they saw her. When she burst through the door, her grandfather was squatting on a blue tarp on the floor skinning a beaver he had caught during the day.

"Close the door!" shouted her mother.

Denny closed the door, and before taking off her parka she blurted the news.

"A teacher was killed by wolves!"

All three adults stopped what they were doing and sat down with Denny at the table to hear the amazing story. Bear attacks on people were commonplace, especially in the summer and fall, and they had all heard stories of wolves killing and eating sled dogs, an easy meal when chained outside to a dog house. But it had been a long time since they had heard of wolves attacking people. The last one either Denny's grandparents could remember was back in the 1950s, when a woman was killed in her village while carrying a bag of groceries home from the general store.

"Better keep an ear and eye out in case they come around here," said Sampson, looking to make sure that his rifle was still leaning beside the door. "Thirty miles not far for a wolf, especially if they follow the river."

After a while, everyone went back to work.

Sampson finished skinning the beaver, and his wife cut up the dark meat for a stew. Nothing went to waste. In the old days, even the teeth were used as amulets worn about the necks of infants. It was believed the teeth instilled the power of industriousness and hard work, a desirable trait in a people who had to live on such a harsh and unforgiving land.

Sampson called his granddaughter.

"Denny, come give your granddaddy a hand."

As he held down one edge of the hide on a board, fur down, he instructed her to nail it. Then he pulled the opposite side of the hide taut across the board so she could nail it down as well. In no time at all, the beaver pelt was properly stretched into a circle and ready to be scraped, the first step in tanning any hide. The work would normally be done outside. But in the winter, when it was so cold and dark outside, both large and small game were often butchered inside the house. Sampson had cut up caribou and moose on the floor dozens of times.

Denny knelt beside her grandfather, watching him scrape the fat from the skin.

"Grandpa, I thought wolves didn't attack people?" she said, trying not to imagine the last terrible moments of the teacher's life, her utter horror when she must have realized what was happening.

"That true most the time," he said without looking up. "But wolves are wild. Everything wild is unpredictable. Take a family dog. One moment it's on its back letting you rub its belly, and the next it attacks a child or somebody else. That dog is a thousand generations removed from its wild ancestors. And yet, some ancient memory of hunting and killing lies just beneath the surface."

Denny nodded. She had heard many stories of dogs attacking children, not only in her own village, but in villages all over. She knew one woman who, as a young girl, had half her face bitten off by sled dogs.

The old man turned the board so he could scrape the hide from a different angle.

"Village dogs in a pack are even worse. Being in a pack erases half of those thousand generations. They turn half wild. Now imagine a wolf, never made to serve men—not even once in all of wolf history—running in a pack, killing to survive, without no mercy and hard as the land itself."

"But why did the *tikaani* kill her?" Denny asked, using the Indian word for wolf. "Why didn't they just catch a moose or a caribou?"

The old man chuckled.

"It not that easy, Granddaughter. Big as the land is, sometimes it's empty, especially in winter. Maybe all the caribou go away someplace else. Maybe them wolves starving. They had to choose between their life and the woman's life."

Deneena was quiet for a few minutes, just watching the way her grandfather meticulously scraped the pelt, careful not to cut the dead animal's skin.

"You remember the word for beaver?" he asked without slowing his work.

"*Tsa'*," Denny replied, properly pronouncing the one-syllable word "chaw."

"Very good. And what about the pelt?"

"I don't think you or grandma ever taught me that one," said Denny.

"The word for skin is *zes*; so the word for beaver pelt is *tsa' zes*," said the old man.

Both were quiet for a long time. Finally, Denny broke the silence.

"There are a lot of wolves in this country. What if they come after me when I'm out on the trail alone?"

The old man stopped, raising his eyes to meet hers.

"Just be wary at all times. You never know what a wild animal is going to do. It don't matter how much respect you show it. A bear may bite you whether you call it bear or Mr. Bear. For the most part, wolves keep to themselves when it comes to people. Sometimes they don't. I was attacked by wolves a long time ago, when I was fifteen. I was alone, just like that teacher—a small, scrawny boy all alone in the great white with nothin' but a single-shot .22 rifle. I thought I was a goner."

"What did you do? How did you escape?" asked Denny.

Just then her mother called out that it was time for supper.

The old man struggled to his feet, placed a hand in the small of his back and groaned.

"I tell you some other time," he said, as he shuffled to the dinner table.

That night, after helping her grandmother wash the dishes and taking a bath in the metal tub, Denny lay in bed and wrote in her diary.

Today a teacher was killed by wolves. I always liked her. All day long I've been thinking about that terrible moment. Did she run? Did she try to fight them off? I don't know what I would have done. I've never been afraid of wolves before, but now I don't know. At school Mary P. was drinking again. I told her it was bad for her baby, but she blew me off like always. Why can't people see the destruction they cause? I mean, people blame the past for their bad decisions, but someday in the future, their choices become the past. Time is a circle in that way. Everyone's always saying how they can't wait to leave the village. I don't feel that way. What would happen if all the young people left? Who would take care of the elders? If only they could see the beauty of this place, instead of what they see on television—all them music videos trying to convince them that life is one giant party if they only lived in a big city. I've been thinking about another poem. I wrote part of it during school today. It doesn't have a title yet. I know it's not important. No one will ever read these. No one even really cares.

> I am beginning to write in our language,
> but it is difficult.
>
> Only elders speak our words,
> and they are forgetting.
>
> There are not many words anyhow.
> They are scattered like clouds,
>
> like salmon in Stepping Creek
> at Tonsina River.
>
> I do not speak like an elder,
> but I hear the voice of a spirit,
> hear it at a distance
> speaking quietly to me.

LAND OF ICE

Dahwdezeldiin' koht'aene kenaege',
ukesdezt'aet.

Yaane' koht'aene yaen',
nekenaege' nadahdelna.

Koht'aene kenaege' k'os nadestaan,
łukae c'ena' ti'taan', Tez'aedzi Na'.

Sii 'e koht'aene k'e kenaes,
Sii ndahwdel'en,
dandiilen
s'dayn'tnel'en.

3

Na' baaghe
River's Edge

The week passed quickly with no sightings of the wolves that had killed the teacher, and Deneena woke up excited on Saturday morning. Her mother had reluctantly agreed that she could snowshoe up to a small log cabin about seven miles back in the mountains to stay the night. She knew how much Denny loved the peace and quiet of the wilderness. Besides, Denny always took one of her school books to read at night.

Denny packed a knapsack with food she'd need for the trip: a couple of moose sausages to roast over a campfire for lunch, a can of chili for dinner, and bacon and biscuits for breakfast. She tossed in a pack of matches, a roll of toilet paper, and a couple extra candles, just in case the oil lamp was empty. On top of everything, she carefully set her diary, along with Anne Frank's *Diary of a Young Girl,* which Ms. Stevens had assigned them to read over the weekend for English and history.

When she was ready to leave, her grandfather handed her the pack.

"I'll come check on you 'round suppertime. Make sure you got a hot pot of tea ready," he said in his grandfatherly tone.

"But, Grandpa, I don't need anyone to check on me."

"I know," whispered the old man, glancing over his shoulder at Delia who was sitting beside her mother on the worn sofa sewing and doing beadwork. "But you momma worried about you. I promised to go check on you. That the only way she let you go."

He winked. He knew she would be safe at the cabin, but Denny's mother worried about a young girl hiking up into the mountains all alone, especially after the wolf attack on the teacher.

"Here, take my rifle," he said, handing it to her. "You know how to shoot it. I got another one in the closet. Here's a few extra bullets."

Denny put the bullets in her parka pocket and slung the rifle over her shoulder.

"Thanks, Grandpa," she said and gave him a hug.

She turned toward her mother when she opened the door to leave.

"See you tomorrow."

Her mother never looked up from her sewing.

Denny loved the long trek into the hills, the solitude, where the only sound was that of her snowshoes and the wind in the trees. Along the way, she saw *deniigi*, a bull moose, far up on a hillside nibbling thin alders and willows. She shot two *ggax*—rabbits—which during winter turned totally white to hide from the many predators that hunted them.

Life was hard at the bottom of the animal food chain.

It took Denny almost three hours to snowshoe to the cabin, which was as cold inside as was the whitened world outside its door. She quickly got a fire going in the belly of the wood stove. While it roared, she unpacked her knapsack. Then she went outside and filled a large pot with packed snow, which she sat on the smoking-hot stove surface. It was only after completing these chores that she sat down at the little table by the small window and began to read Anne Frank's diary.

She got up after reading thirty pages to put another log in the stove and to check on her water. All the snow had melted, leaving only a few inches of water in the bottom. She stepped outside and added more snow to the pot. It was a slow process, melting snow for drinking and cooking water, but it was less strenuous than hauling water at eight pounds a gallon. After poking the fire to settle the hissing and popping logs, Denny finally took off her parka and sat down to resume reading. Several pages in, something outside the window caught her eye.

A wolf was in the front yard snuffling in the fresh snow around a deadfall. He was jet black, except for one gray-white ear. Denny had seen wolves before, and she knew that while most wolves were gray and mottled, some were all black. But for this black wolf to have one discolored ear was rare—one in a million.

Suddenly, it stopped, gazed intently at the ground, pricked its ears, and pounced, catlike. It didn't catch whatever it was chasing. She watched as the wolf spun about, snuffled in the snow and pounced again. After several failed attempts, the wolf finally caught a small mouse. From where she sat, she could see the thin tail hanging from the wolf's mouth. She leaned closer to the window, knocking over a salt shaker. The sharp sound startled the wolf, and he ran away.

For the next half hour Denny busily worked on writing a new poem, wondering why the wolf was all alone.

That evening, right on time, Sampson arrived on his snowmobile, the bright headlight glaring through the window. He shut off the engine, and darkness and quiet returned to the valley. As promised, Denny had a hot pot of tea on the wood stove. She poured him a cup when he sat down at the table after hanging his hat and parka on a hook.

"The trail was good," he said, warming his hands around the cup. "I made it here in less than twenty minutes. Saw two moose on the way up."

Denny told her grandfather about the wolf she had seen out front pouncing on a little mouse.

He laughed on hearing her description.

"People always think wolves just eat moose and caribou, but a big part of their diet is small things like mice. It take lots of *dluuni* to fill a wolf belly."

"Grandpa," said Deneena.

The old man could tell from her tone that she had something serious to say.

"Almost all of the other kids at school drink all the time. They even smoke marijuana when they can get it. They always make fun of me when I don't do it with them. I want to fit in. I want them to like me, but I want them to like me for me, for who I am."

Sampson peered out the small window into the darkness outside. Denny could tell he was thinking about what to say. Elders were like that, taking their time to say something. She waited.

Finally he spoke.

"What *they* do, what *you* do—it not a matter of legal or not legal; not even a matter of right or wrong. It about being true to yourself, about deciding your *own* path. People are like rivers, and the hours of our days flow to the sea. But no two rivers are the same, and no river is today what it was last month or last year. It always trying to find new channels, shifting in its gravel bed, hurling itself against boulders and trying to undercut steep banks. Some people are content to follow the course set before them. Life easy that way. Others, like you, jump their banks, daring to be different. Like rivers, people end up at the same place, but how we get there is what makes us who we are."

Denny nodded as if she understood. But she wondered if she was too young to understand what her grandfather was saying. Such knowledge, she thought, comes only from having lived a long life, from long awareness. She was only a girl, she thought as she nodded with a kind of dawning of understanding, the way geese flying above clouds and mountains must be vaguely aware that the world is round.

The old man continued, slowly.

"*You* have to decide who you want to be and what will make you happy. There is nothing you *must* be. There is nothing you *must* do. And despite all them commercials on television, there is nothing you *must* have. If you ask me, finding your own happiness in a hard world is all that means anything. Happiness isn't someplace else, and it don't come from a new car or a big house or fancy clothes or computer games. That snowmobile outside don't make me happy, but at my age, it gets me into the woods, which makes my life worth living. Having lots of money and things can't make you happy. It comes from *here*," he said, thumping his fist against his chest.

Denny scooted out from her chair and hugged him around his neck for a long time.

"*Tsin'aen*," she whispered and kissed him on his coarse cheek. "Thank you, Grandpa."

That night, after Sampson left on the snowmobile for the village, Denny thought about what he had said earlier in the week about how wolves sometimes go hungry, and how that hunger forces them to do things they wouldn't otherwise do. She kept thinking about the lone wolf hunting little *dluuni*, such a small meal for a wolf. After a while, she got up and threw one of her rabbits out in front of the cabin—a gift.

Denny read for another hour or so and worked on one of the many puzzles stacked on a shelf before she finally climbed into the bed in the loft, which was much warmer than the downstairs. She lay in the dark, listening to the sound of wood popping, hoping to hear the wolf outside, and wondering if it could get inside the cabin.

In the morning, after she rebuilt a fire in the wood stove and added snow to the pot for coffee, Denny looked out the frosted window and saw that the rabbit was gone. Fresh wolf tracks littered the snow where it had been.

She smiled.

After a breakfast of bacon, biscuits, and two cups of tea, Denny swept the floor, made the bed, carried in an armful of firewood for the next visit, closed the damper on the wood stove, and while the cabin cooled, she wrote in her diary.

Dear Diary,
I just LOVE Anne Frank's diary! From now on, I'm going to address you as Nellie, the way Anne called her diary Kitty. It's a girl's name that means black bear. It's normally spelled nel'ii. It makes me feel like I'm writing to someone real, like someone really cares and understands. Anne wrote a lot about trying to get along with her parents, especially her mother, who didn't seem to understand her at all. That's exactly how I feel. Sometimes I don't think my mother loves me at all. She's always saying, "Why can't you be more like the other girls in the village?" But if she knew even half of the bad things they do, she wouldn't say that. Grandpa says I'm fine the way I am. I wrote this poem at the cabin after seeing a wolf outside. I used a little poetic license with some stuff. So sue me! I think it's the prettiest little poem I ever wrote.
Yours,
Denny

On Feet of Clouds

A cloud arrives
quiet and gray
as the wolf
hunting field mice
in the frosted meadow
outside my cabin door.

LONE WOLVES

Yanlaey Kae

Yanlaey lunatatez'aan
ghaetl' 'eł baa
k'e tikaani
c'ukatezyaa dluuni
yii cen zogh
'an hwnax hwdatnetaani

4

Ceyiige' gha tene
Spirit of the Trail

As Deneena walked through the village on her way home from the cabin in the hills, her pack and rifle slung over a shoulder, which was not an unusual sight in a village, she saw a man approaching. A dog dashed out from its little yard and barked at the man, who kicked it hard. The dog yelped and scuttled home, favoring one leg, with its tail tucked between its legs. When the man was close, Denny recognized him as her father. It was the first time she had seen him in almost a year.

When they passed, her father looked away, as if something else caught his attention, and continued without stopping or without saying a word. Denny limped home feeling a lot like that wounded dog.

She had barely walked through the door of her house when Sampson got up from the small table and put on his hat and parka and gloves.

"Wanna go run the dogs with me?"

"I just walked seven miles," replied Denny. "I'm tired and hungry."

The old man shrugged his shoulders.

"How hard is it to stand on the back of a sled?"

Denny smiled.

"Can't beat that kind of logic, Grandpa," she said.

"Tell you what," said Sampson, "you get yourself a little something to eat and a cup of hot coffee while I hook up the team. That should take a while."

Denny agreed.

While the old man hooked the dogs to the sled, she made a sandwich and drank two cups of coffee, occasionally looking out the window to make sure her grandfather was okay. She worried about him exerting himself too much. Not long after that, both dog team and snowmobile were following the frozen river, the tiny village behind them. In a picket-fenced cemetery on a hill above the huddled village, ghosts watched from their little painted houses or from behind Russian Orthodox crosses.

Two hours later, the dogs were resting while Denny and her grandfather stood beside a campfire, the old coffee pot perched at the edge of the flames.

"Time to learn," said Sampson, pointing at the aluminum pot. "What the word for coffee?"

"*Guuxi*," answered Deneena, so effortlessly that she surprised herself.

"Correct," replied the old man. "But do you know *why* we call it that?"

Denny thought for a moment, searching her memory.

"No," she finally replied, a bit deflated for not knowing.

Sampson reached inside his parka and pulled out a biscuit wrapped in tinfoil.

"It not really a word in our language, you know. It really an English word," he said, unwrapping the biscuit and taking a bite. "First white man come into this country long time ago and offers an Indian a cup of hot coffee. The Indian drinks it, says it good, and asks what it called. The white man he say *coffee* and gives him some grounds to take with him. That Indian goes home and makes some for his people who ask him what it called. That Indian, who didn't speak English very well, he say *goo-kee*. And that what we still call it."

Denny laughed.

"Is that true, Grandpa?"

"Cross my heart," said Sampson, making the sign of a cross over his parka with his biscuit-clutching hand. "We have lots of words like that, like oatmeal, which we call *utniil*."

Just then a camprobber flew down from a tree limb, snatched a crumb on the ground, and flew away. Actually a common gray jay, the bird had a penchant for stealing food from camps and cabins, which had earned it its nickname. In the interior, they are almost as ubiquitous as the raven.

"I ever tell you how *stakalbaey* got his face?" asked the old man, referring to the little thief.

"I don't think so."

Sampson took another bite of the biscuit and tossed what little remained toward the tree, a gift to the bird, who flew down and snatched it.

"Long time ago, Camprobber and Woodpecker were friends," he began, but then stopped. "I ever tell you the word for woodpecker?"

"Isn't it *cen'łkatl'i?*" she asked.

"You remembered. Good," said Sampson. "Where was I? One day they got into an argument. Woodpecker got so mad he grabbed Camprobber by the neck and shoved his face into their campfire. That camprobber's face all covered with ash. When Woodpecker try to fly away, Camprobber grabbed him by his long tail feathers and held on until all them long tail feathers were pulled out. That's how come camprobbers have ashen spots on their face and why woodpeckers got no long tail feathers."

Denny thought about the story while she fed the dogs. She had heard similar stories from her grandfather and grandmother and other elders—stories about the world around them, how it is ordered, how things and places came to be, and most importantly, how people should live in that world.

"Grandpa," she said, tossing some small pieces of wood on the fire, "I saw my father today."

She was quiet for a while before she spoke again.

"How come he doesn't want anything to do with me?"

This was a subject that Denny never talked about, though the old man, by his manner, seemed to know how much it hurt her. All her life, he had watched Denny's father ignore her whenever he returned to the village to visit his family or to attend a potlatch for someone who had died. Sometimes, he just came home to feel the safety of the familiar, even though he hated the village. As far back as he could remember, the man, who was almost always drunk, had never said a single word to his young daughter, never sent a birthday card or Christmas present.

"I mean, whenever he's here, he acts like I'm invisible . . . like I'm a ghost or something."

Sampson looked at faraway mountains, the sun already dipping below the crest.

"You daddy got his own problems," he said. "You not one of them. He doesn't know who he is. It always been that way for him because he half Indian and half White. That where you got your blue eyes. But because of that, he never fit in nowhere. People in the village say, 'You not really Indian.' Some of his own relatives say that, even though they know better. People in the city say, 'You not really White.' It a hard thing for a man to never fit in nowhere, to not belong. Your father always restless, always look-ing for something else . . . something more from his life. Maybe just acceptance. The village wasn't big enough for him. After you was born, he left you momma and moved to the city to make his name. But the city swallowed him. Yessir, the city chewed him up and swallowed him whole."

"What does that mean?" asked Denny.

"Everyone always saying how they want to leave the village, always saying how good it would be to go somewhere else . . ."

Denny thought about the other kids at school and how they were always saying things like that.

" . . . But that other place don't want them . . . nothing there but lots of steel and concrete and bright lights and loneliness. Sorrow stands in the shadows and greets them with open arms, holds them so tight they can't breathe. Before you know it, all them dreams turn to dust, and all that's left is bitterness and ha-tred—hatred for the self for not being able to find a place in the world. Sometimes the heart fills up with that hate, and the only thing that settles it is the bottle. That not always the case, but it was for you daddy."

Sampson bent down and poured a cup of coffee.

"Want some?" he asked.

Denny shook her head.

"But why does he take it out on me?"

"It not you he hates. He hates himself. You represent anoth-er failure in his life—his failure to be a husband and a father. Just one more thing on a long list of failures. His pain is deep. He is ashamed of himself, and shame is a terrible thing. Your fa-ther's anger make him want to tear both worlds to pieces. You just caught in the middle."

Denny was saddened on learning of the pain that must be in-side the father she barely knew.

"But I'm a good person. He'd . . . he'd love me if he only knew me."

"Of course he would," replied the old man with a sympathetic smile.

"I . . . I feel like . . . like I *need* him to love me or else I'll never know who I am."

Sampson turned to Denny and took her by the shoulders, pulled her close, and looked her in the eyes.

"You can't find yourself by finding somebody else," he said.

Denny tried to wipe away the tears sliding down her face.

"I . . . I don't know who I am!" she sobbed.

"But I know who you are. You my granddaughter, and I love you."

Neither said a word for a while. Denny broke a few pieces of wood over her knee for the fire, while Sampson checked the sled and the rigging.

"I been thinking," he said, looking up from his work, "there's a dog race coming up next weekend. I think you should be in it."

"But, Grandpa, do you really think I'm ready for a race? Do you think I have a chance of winning?"

"It not a long race. And it don't matter if you win or lose. What matters is that you try. In our way a person doesn't have to beat out others to be strong. The strength of one is a source of strength for the entire village. A great hunter is great because he brings home food not only for his family but for others too. He shares his success. That a big difference in the world today. Everyone always got to be better than everyone else, stand above them. Everyone always got to beat down the next person for everything. Everyone want to take what is yours for themselves. It every man for himself. But that no good way to live. Better to belong to a community. Better to help each other. That way others help you when you are down or weak or old like me."

Denny recalled how her grandfather always gave some of his moose, or caribou, or salmon to other families in the village, especially to those who had many children or who were unable to hunt for themselves any longer.

Sampson knelt close to the fire, warming his hands above the flames.

"I tell you a story that my grandmother used to tell me. A long time ago, back in *yanida'a*, a young man from a village was walking in the woods when he saw a mouse carrying a large fish egg in his mouth. The mouse was struggling to climb over a log fallen across its path. The man bent down and picked up the mouse real gentle and placed it on the other side of the log. The mouse scurried into the brush and was gone.

"That winter was a hard one for the people of that man's village. Halfway through the coldest and darkest time, the food supplies run out, and the people were starving. Surely, they would not survive."

"But one day, while the young man out looking for food, he came on a tiny house with smoke coming from a tiny smoke-hole. Just then a small voice told the man to turn around three times with his eyes closed. The man did this and became so small he could fit through the tiny door. Inside the warm house stood a man in a brown fur coat."

'I have been expecting you, *cii*,' said the strange man. 'Come and sit down.'

"The young man sat down and listened."

'Your people have no food. It has been a very hard winter for them. But I will help you,' said the man in the brown fur coat."

"The strange man brought out a small pack, which he began to fill with dried berries and fish meat and other things to eat. He gave the pack to the young man from the village, who asked why he was helping him."

'Last summer you helped me. I was carrying home a large fish egg for my family, and you helped me across a fallen tree. Because you helped me *then*, I will help you *now*.'

"Suddenly, the young man remembered helping the little mouse, and he understood this was the same mouse. He went outside and became big again, but the pack of food remained small."

'I thank you for this gift, but it is not enough to feed my people.'

The mouse man replied, 'When you return to your village, leave the pack outside for the night and sing this song, which I will now teach you.'

"The man did as he was instructed, and the next morning the little pack turned into a large one full of food. It was so heavy the man could barely lift it. The young man had saved his village from starvation, all because he had helped a smaller, weaker animal."

"You see, Granddaughter, love and compassion for others is the only way to live. Kindness is repaid with kindness."

Though Denny had never heard the story before, she recognized its universal message. She looked at the dogs curled up and resting after their supper. She looked at the sled and then down the trail, a slight wind blowing her long, black hair into her blue eyes.

"I don't know if I'm ready for a race," she said, feeling excited and anxious at the same time. "What if I come in last and make a fool of myself?"

"Listen to me," her grandfather said in a way that always meant *Pay attention to what I'm about to say. This is important!* "Never run away from what you really want to do just because you unsure of how it will turn out. If you fail while daring to do something great, then you have not failed at all. When you risk nothing, you risk everything. When I first started mushing, I didn't win no races for three years, but I kept tryin' anyhow."

"I don't know," Denny repeated with a look of apprehension.

"Well, let me know soon," replied Sampson. "There's only a few days left to sign up."

On the way home, Denny thought about the mouse story, reciting it in her memory so she could write it down in her diary the way she wrote down every story he told her. She also thought about the race as the dogs pulled the sled along a well-marked trail on the wide and frozen river, passing the little cemetery perched on the hill above the village—the full moon rising above it looking like an ivory eye carved in the black face of the sky.

That evening, while her grandmother was doing beadwork at the small kitchen table and her mother was cooking the rabbit she had brought home earlier in the day, Denny sat cross-legged on her narrow bed, writing down the beautiful story her grandfather had told her. She was careful not to forget a single word. When she was done, she turned the pages to write a new entry in her diary.

Dear Nellie,

I had a long talk with grandpa about my dad. I never talk about him, not even to mother, but I think about him all the time. It's like I have this giant hole inside me. I mean, if anyone in the world is meant to love you, it has to be your parents, right? How can a father not love his child? I'm half of him; he's half of me. People always say how much I look like him. What does he think when he sees me? Does he feel any-thing? Does he even see me? I don't understand at all. Sometimes I get really sad when I think about it. Sometimes I get mad. Grandpa thinks I'm ready to enter a race, but I'm not as certain as he is. I know all the other kids want to move away as soon as they can, but I love it here. I can understand why Grandpa loves it so much. I love it, too.
Yours,

Denny

Riversong

I never want to leave this land.
All of my ancestors are buried here,
listening to riversong
from picket-fenced graves,
their wind-borne spirits
linking past and present.

When I finally fall to pieces
this is where my pieces will fall.

After washing dishes and taking her nightly bath, Denny read the last pages of Anne Frank's diary. She learned from the epilogue that Anne and her fellow occupants of the "secret annex" were eventually discovered and sent away to Nazi concentration camps. In the last sentence of the last page, Denny read with dismay that Anne died seven months later at Bergen-Belsen concentration camp, where Jewish prisoners were murdered because they were Jewish.

She closed the book and sat for a long time with the book on her lap, looking at the cover through tear-filled eyes, caressing the spine and pages, trying to imagine Anne's life . . . and death. She couldn't fathom life in one of those terrible places. She and Anne were almost the same age and shared many of the same teenage concerns, like boys, and the struggle to figure out who you are supposed to be, and most importantly, how to deal with the uncertain relationships to mother and father. After a while, Denny got up, put the book in her school backpack, pulled out her own diary from its hiding place—its secret annex—and sat on her bed scribbling a postscript with a purple-colored pen.

P.S.: I HATE the end of this book! Our teacher didn't tell us anything about how Anne dies at the end! She was almost the same age as I am. How could that happen? How could people do that to each other? Where's the kindness that Grandfather talks about? What kind of god allows such terrible things to happen? Was all of Anne's suffering and sacrifice for nothing? She never even got a chance to be a girl. She never got a chance to really live. Grandpa's right; I should enter that race. If he could do it, then I can do it! Carpe diem!

5

Hnae ghu' 'aen
Words Have Teeth

During breakfast the next morning, Deneena told her grandfather that she would enter the race.

"Good for you!" said Sampson, slapping his knee. "A chip off the old block. I'll call my friend and get you signed up."

Denny's mother stopped what she was doing.

"What's that about a race?" she asked, with her arms across her chest.

"I'm going to be in a dogsled race this weekend," replied Denny happily. "Grandpa says I'm ready."

Delia glared at her father.

"Why do you fill her mind with such notions? She's a girl, Dad. She shouldn't be racing dogs or hiking up to cabins all by herself, for god's sake! It's too dangerous."

"But, Mom, you're always telling me that a woman can be anything she wants to be," said Denny. "You're always telling me to believe in myself. Were you lying?"

"No," replied her mother. "But you need to act more like a girl, or you'll end up all alone."

Denny thought her mother was really talking about herself. She knew that her mother's generation had, for the most part, turned their backs on the old ways, wanting their children, instead, to fit in with the new world . . . the white world.

"You need to stop hanging around with dogs in the woods and make some friends. Why can't you wear a dress once in a while? And would it kill you to put on some make-up? Why can't you be more like that Mary Paniaq?"

Denny bit her lip, literally. She wanted to scream. She wanted to throw something.

Be like Mary! If Mother only knew what I know, would she think a pregnant, pot-smoking, alcoholic teenager with a total disregard for her baby is better than me?

"What about what I want?" she yelled, almost in tears. "What about who I want to be? Maybe I don't want to be like *you*!"

On hearing the last words, her mother let her jaw slack and her arms fell to her side.

Denny grabbed her parka and school bag. She wheeled around in the open doorway.

"I *am* going to be in the race! You can't stop me!" she shouted before slamming the door.

On the walk to school Denny felt bad. She realized how hard it had to be for her mother, raising a child alone, living with her parents in a small village offering but few good jobs, living where everyone knows your business. Denny remembered how Anne had written in her diary that she hated her mother but how, by the end of the book, she came to understand how much it would hurt her mother to read something like that from her own daughter.

"I don't hate her," she said to the deaf trees. "I just want her to love me for who I am."

At school, while standing behind the building during lunch break, Denny told everyone that she was going to enter the dog race.

"That's crazy!" said Johnny Shaginoff, taking a drag on a cigarette.

"Girls don't mush," said Mary Paniaq, taking a sip from her flask.

Norman Fury rolled his eyes and shook his head in disbelief.

"You don't have a chance in hell," he said.

Only Silas Charley said anything encouraging.

"I'll go," he whispered, when everyone else was talking about something else.

"What'd you say?" asked Deneena.

"I'll go watch you race."

After everyone else went into the building, Denny grabbed Silas by his jacket and stopped him in front of the main doors.

"How come you're being nice to me?" she asked.

"I just like watching dog races. My uncle used to race."

"But you've never been nice to me before. I mean, whenever you guys are all drunk or high, all you ever do is make fun of me, saying how I don't have a father, how I'm such a tomboy, or how I'm such an old fashioned goody-two-shoes."

Silas leaned close to Denny.

"I'll tell you a little secret," he whispered. "I don't really do none of those bad things. I just want people to think I do, so they'll like me. That's all."

"But I've seen you do that stuff a hundred times," replied Denny.

"The way I see it, there's three ways to deal with peer pressure," he said, with both hands in his pockets. "You can join in and screw up your life or maybe someone else's life. Mary's doing enough of that for anyone."

Denny nodded slowly, impressed that Silas saw the same thing she did.

"You can walk away," Silas continued, "which says to the others you think you're better than they are. Maybe this works, but you won't have too many friends. No one likes to be reminded they act like idiots."

Denny recognized that this was her approach. She didn't mean for people to think that she thought she was better than they were.

"And then there's *my* way. I'm what you might call a *faker*. I *pretend* to take a swig or a puff. Like, at a party, I pour out my glass of booze, little by little, when no one is looking. No one ever notices; they just figure I must have drunk it all. I know . . . it sounds lame. But that way, I fit in without messing up my life. The way I figure, I'm not hurting no one . . . just wasting a lot of booze, that's all."

Denny grinned. She did a similar thing with brussel sprouts when she was a little girl, hiding them in her napkin when her mother wasn't looking so that her mother would think she ate them all and praise her.

"I hadn't thought of that before," she said.

"Well, now you know," replied Silas, with a smile that would disarm a snarling wolf. "Besides, I've never actually said a bad thing about you. I just nodded whenever the others did, but really I was just moving to the music in my head."

Denny laughed, a little uncertainly.

Just then the fourth-period bell rang.

When Denny walked through the cabin door after school, her grandfather was working on the sled in the living room. The sled was upside down, with the bottom of the runners facing up.

"What you working on grandpa?" she asked, removing her school pack and parka.

"Sanding the runners. Gotta keep them smooth. Sleds go faster without nicks and gouges. You need every chance for the race."

Deneena knew that rocks hurt the runners. Rocks were not normally a problem on the snow-covered trail itself, but sometimes a musher had to drive on or across a road to get to the trail.

"Nowadays, racers put Teflon strips on the bottom and they replace them whenever they get bad. But I like the old way—wood on snow," he said while leaning close and looking down the long runner, checking for rough spots.

He sanded a spot and then ran his fingers along the place.

"Good as new," he said, smiling. "Come feel for yourself."

Denny ran her hand along the entire length.

"Nice job, Grandpa."

"I got to put a coat of lacquer on the wood to seal it. Wanna help?"

While the two worked, one on each side of the upturned sled, Sampson taught his granddaughter the words for all the parts.

"The sled we call *xał*."

Denny repeated the word, pronouncing it the way the old man did: hoth.

"We call the runners *xał tl'aaxi*," said Sampson, while thinly applying the lacquer with a brush.

Denny repeated the name.

"The basket we call *xał yii*."

By "basket" the old man meant the part of the sled in which cargo is carried—any cargo: people, supplies, fuel, firewood, moose or caribou meat, sometimes even a sick or exhausted dog. Anything that will fit inside the frame.

Sampson grabbed one of the short braces that gave the sled strength. "These stanchions we call *xał dzaade'*."

Denny committed it to memory, the way she cataloged every word her grandfather ever taught her.

"What is the word for the handle?" she asked, pointing to it.

"We call that *xał daten'*. There is a word for every single part of a sled, just like there are words for every part of a snowshoe.

"And the main line? Is there a word for that?" asked Denny.

Sampson chuckled.

"I just tell you, there a word for everything, even the littlest part. You don't listen very well. But then, you Gramma always telling me I don't listen to anything she says. The main line is called *titl'uule'*."

Denny pronounced the new word aloud.

"Very good. Don't forget that spot over there," her grandfather said, pointing his brush at a small place that Denny had missed.

Denny carefully applied lacquer to the spot, drawing the brush in long, slow strokes.

"Grandpa," she said. "Do you think I have a chance with an old sled like this? I mean, nowadays, racers use high-tech, lightweight sleds. This one has to be almost twice as heavy."

"This a *great* sled," said the old man gripping a stanchion and giving the entire sled a shake. "I built it myself. Very strong. Can take a beating."

Denny thought she might have hurt her grandfather's feelings.

"It's a wonderful sled, Grandpa. But all those racers have super-light sleds made of high-tech materials. They even got satellite cell phones. Most of them have business sponsors to pay for everything, and they have patches and the names of their sponsors sewn all over their expensive jackets. I don't have any of that stuff. I'm just an Indian girl from an Indian village with a bunch of Indian dogs."

Sampson set down his brush and stood up straight.

"Let me tell you something," he said, almost angrily. "You gotta be proud of who you are and where you come from. Let me tell you something else. The person who wins, he don't win because he has the fanciest equipment or rich supporters. Those things can only take you so far. What matters is *ciz'aani*—heart. You got to have *heart* to win. You got to want something so bad that you can't give up, not even an option. When things seem to go really bad, when failure knocks you down and kicks you in the gut, that's when heart matters most. You gotta dig deep inside yourself to find the strength, to find out what kind of person you are. Yes, the person who wins sometimes has the best equipment. But just as often, the winner is the person who wants it most. You, Grand-daughter, have a big heart. Maybe the biggest. I see that in you. That why I'm giving you this sled."

"But I don't have any of the things other racers have. People will laugh at me."

"It don't matter what other people think. I teach you that already. Only heart matters and that never changes just because we got television or cell phones. People give up too easy nowadays. Look around the village and you can see that. You got to work hard for something to appreciate it. Only things that are earned from hard work and sweat mean anything. Don't quit just because something is hard. You kids gotta learn that."

That night, as Denny lay in her bed thinking about what her grandfather had said to her and about the coming race, she gazed at the sled glowing dimly in the yellow light from the flames of the wood stove—the flickering light casting dancing shadows on the walls. Sometime after midnight, Denny pulled out her diary and turned on the little nightlight beside her bed.

Dear Nellie,

I think I learned something important tonight. Grandpa talked about how most people don't appreciate things that come too easy to them. I think I understand what he meant. All the time I see people in the village get free money. They go buy expensive new snowmobiles, and within a year the machine is a piece of junk because they didn't take care of it at all, because they know they'll get more free money one day. I remember when I was ten, and I really wanted a new bike. Mother made me work all winter to save up enough money to buy it myself. I did all kinds of little jobs to make money, and then I bought that bike. I took such good care of it, because I knew how much work went into getting it. It was special. Grandpa's sled may be old-fashioned, but it's beautiful because he made it with his own two hands. His sweat is in

the wooden heart of that sled. There's power in that. I wrote another
poem. It's corny. No need to explain it. Sometimes, a poem's meaning
is obvious.
Yours,
Denny

Portrait of the Artist as a Teenage Girl

Although I am nobody
writing lines to poems
no one will ever know,
I do not fail to cast
a tiny shadow
on the
snow.

p.s. Grandpa also talked about having heart. He said I have the big-
gest heart. I wrote another poem. Seems like good words to live by . . .

Heart

Heart is like a mirror—
bury it in mud
let it rust and grow with moss
and no more will it reflect the world's beauty.

Ciz'aani

Ciz'aani ke' uyii na'stnal'aeni—
kiighiłtaen tah bestl'es
k'ena na'stnal'aeni tsaan' 'eł kołii kae dlaadon'
'eł na'stnal'aeni galdiine' niic nen' kasuundze'.

6

Ts'itk'ey dzaen yuuł
A Day's Journey

On the last day of school before Christmas vacation, Denny left before the last period so that she could get the dogs on the trail early enough. She wanted the pace of the thirty mile journey to the village upriver—where the teacher was killed—to be leisurely, not overly tiring for the dogs before the race the next day. Sampson followed on his snowmobile.

Denny's mother didn't go.

"Go run your stupid race," she had said from the porch, while Denny was finishing hitching the dogs to the sled. "When you lose, maybe you get that nonsense out of your head, once and for all."

"Thanks for the support!" Denny shouted sarcastically when she pulled the snow hook and commanded the dogs to run.

Her grandmother waved goodbye from the frosted window.

Sampson started his snowmobile. He waved to his wife and shouted goodbye.

"*Xonahang 'aat'!*"

Halfway to the village, the trail left the frozen river and meandered through the woods because that stretch of the river was

63

largely unfrozen. As Denny made her way through the forest, another musher approached from the opposite direction.

Denny recognized the man.

It was Lincoln Lincoln. He was from her village and a good musher, just like his older brother, Bassille. Bassille had died two years prior when his team broke through thin ice on the river and never made it out. Dogs, musher, and sled . . . all yanked beneath the ice by the current.

"Trail!" yelled Lincoln above the din of the barking dogs.

Deneena knew the command, a request to yield the right of way. Snowy forest trails are typically too narrow for mushers to pass easily. One musher has to drive off the trail to make room for the other—a kind of sledding courtesy.

"Haw!" shouted Denny.

The lead dog guided the rest of the team off the left side of the trail and waited for Lincoln's team to pass.

About an hour later, without incident, Denny and her grandfather arrived in the village. They stayed at Joseph Yazzie's house for the night. Joseph was Sampson's first cousin. After the dogs were fed and bedded down for the night, all on piles of straw to keep them off the ground, Denny came inside for a supper of Joseph's deep-fried burbot, a freshwater cod, which he had caught while out ice fishing earlier in the day.

"Good *ts'anyae*," Joseph said during the meal, using the Indian word for burbot. "Poor man's lobster."

"What's that mean?" asked Denny, looking inquisitively at her grandfather.

"That what they say about the white meat of burbot," replied Sampson. "They say it taste like lobster. But I don't know if that true 'cause I never ate lobster."

"That's because you're a poor man," said Joseph with a big smile.

All three laughed.

"It was hard out there today, standing around on the ice checking my holes and waiting for fish to bite," said Joseph. "I'm getting too old for that kind of thing. Better to sit inside where it warm and drink *tsaey*. That's *tea*, in case you didn't know," he said to Denny.

"I know what *tsaey* is," Denny replied defiantly.

Sampson interrupted.

"We both getting old," he said.

"How old are you now, Cousin," asked Joseph.

"Seventy-six, which means you seventy-five."

Joseph Yazzie leaned back in his creaking chair.

"We getting old, I tell you what," he said, and then got up to stoke the dying fire and pour a cup of hot tea from a blue pot on the stove.

The next day, more than a dozen different dog teams crowded into the village for the race. All the mushers, except Denny, were men. Denny was checking the rigging and the booties on each dog when Silas Charley arrived on his father's snowmobile.

"Told you I'd be here," he said, after turning off the engine and raising the visor on his helmet.

Denny smiled.

"I'm glad you're here. I'm really nervous."

"Just run the race. Don't worry about everyone else. You're pretty good. I've watched you," said Silas.

"Thanks," replied Denny.

Just then her grandfather came over.

"It's time," he said. "You need to get over to the starting area."

He helped Denny tie on her race bib with a large, black number 7 on the front and back.

"That a lucky number," he said.

A drawing determined the order in which each musher would leave the starting gate. Denny was sixth, about halfway among the teams. In sled racing, each team starts several minutes after the previous one, providing room on the trail. Unlike with a marathon or other foot race, officials mark the start and finish time of every team. Whoever completes the race in the shortest time is the winner. Sometimes a team "scratches," or pulls out of the race, if they encounter an insurmountable problem, like a broken runner.

The race course was a simple route. It went upriver for about seven miles, turned off into the woods and followed a slough back to the river where the race started. Mushers were to run the loop twice. Locals lined the trail in places, sitting on their snowmobiles or lawn chairs, drinking hot coffee, and cheering for their favorite musher, often a relative. Some spectators built bonfires around which children and adults alike roasted hot dogs or marshmallows.

Silas waved at Denny when she passed.

"You go, girl!" he yelled.

After finishing the first loop, Denny had moved up to fifth place. On the wide-open stretch along the frozen river, she pulled ahead of another team and was in fourth. By the time she emerged from the slough a half mile before the finish line, she was in third place, with no team close enough behind to seriously challenge her. Denny was gaining on the team in second. With a little more distance to the finish line, she might have passed it. Out of a dozen teams in the race, all led by men, 16-year-old-rookie Deneena Yazzie finished in third place. She smiled proudly when officials announced her name on the loudspeaker, handing her a small trophy and a check for $400.

"I told you that you ready. Didn't I tell you?" said Sampson in a voice hoarse from cheering. "You a real racer now. I'm proud of you."

Denny hugged her grandfather, with her trophy in one hand and the prize check in the other. She wondered what her mother would say when she told her the good news.

Afterward, Denny and Silas bumped fists to celebrate.

"You were real good out there," he said, looking at the snow-covered ground.

"Thanks," replied Denny.

They stood in an awkward silence for a moment, neither really looking at the other.

"I gotta get going," said Denny. "We're having supper at my second cousin's house."

"Yeah, I gotta get home myself. See you back in the village."

The next morning, hours before sun-up, Denny and her grandfather set off for home beneath a star-raddled sky with the northern lights streaking overhead. The thermometer outside Joseph's cabin had read -10. Somewhere along the thirty-mile ride back to their village, Sampson got his snowmobile stuck in overflow, where water from beneath the ice rises and mixes with the deep snow on the surface of the ice to create slush. He had been playing around, speeding far ahead of Denny and her dog team, and making his own trail in deep snow off the packed, main trail, when he found himself knee-deep in the heavy slush. Concealed as it was by snow and darkness, he had not seen the ensnaring trap until it was too late.

At first, his momentum helped him to slog through the overflow, but the engine quickly bogged down, and the machine wouldn't budge no matter how much he gunned the throttle. A snowmobile on a firm trail is already a heavy thing to lift or move. Stuck as it was in deep overflow, the machine was far too heavy for a single man to move, no matter how strong. But if he left the stranded machine in the slush for too long, it could freeze solid where it sat, and then he'd have a much bigger problem.

Knowing this, Sampson yanked and pulled and tugged at the front skis and at the black handle at the rear. With all his might, he tried to manhandle the machine out from the quicksand-like mix of snow and water, until his heart was pounding like a potlatch drum. His gloves were soaked from reaching into the icy water. His pants were soaked clear up past his knees. He couldn't feel his frozen fingers or toes.

Suddenly, he felt a stabbing pain in his left arm, like an ice pick in the crook of his elbow. A cold sweat drenched his body, and he felt dizzy and nauseous, twice almost vomiting. He steadied himself with one hand on the black snowmobile seat, the other held against his chest, as if he could somehow control his heart's erratic beating.

In the distance, he could see his granddaughter coming around the river bend.

Just then, Sampson collapsed, his world turning as dark as a wintry night.

From faraway, Denny saw her grandfather fall to the snow. She shouted to the dogs to go faster. When she was close, Denny stopped the sled near the stranded snowmobile, but still on the packed trail. She quickly set the snow brake and ran to the crumpled old man.

Sampson was regaining consciousness, trying to get up from his knees. Denny helped him to his unsteady feet.

"Are you okay?" she asked.

Sampson's face was white and drenched in sweat. He didn't answer.

"Grandpa?" she said again, "Are you alright?"

Sampson turned to his granddaughter, speaking so softly she barely heard him.

"Take me home," he whispered.

Denny helped her grandfather into the belly of the sled and covered him with her own parka to keep him warm. In a panic, she pulled the snow hook and shouted the command to go. The dogs yanked so hard that Denny almost lost her grip, nearly falling off the back of the sled. But she held on, yelling through the darkness to go faster.

"Mush!" she yelled over and over again.

The dogs ran as fast as their legs could move, their pink tongues flapping from their slobbering mouths as they pushed their muscles and lungs to their limits.

Denny looked down at her grandfather whenever she could take her eyes off the trail.

"Hang in there, Grandpa! Just a little further," she reassured him, though they were still far from the village and her voice was not as certain her words.

"Mush!" she yelled. "Faster!"

Sampson looked up at his granddaughter's worried face, blinking at the sharp-pointed stars and trees tilting over the river when the trail passed close to a steep bank. Soaking wet as he was, he could no longer feel his body.

Denny shivered without her parka, protected from the wind and cold only by a sweater, her teeth chattering.

Out of the corner of her eye, against the whiteness of snow occasionally brightened by the night sky, she saw something running through the scraggily trees parallel to the trail. She strained to make out the shadowy figure in the darkness. It was the black wolf with one gray ear, the one she had seen at the cabin. She was certain that it was the same wolf. He was running *with* them, following alongside, loping easily through the deep snow.

Denny marveled at his strength.

"Mush!" she yelled to the dogs.

"Faster!" she pleaded through tears, turning her eyelashes to ice.

But somewhere along the wide and frozen river, beneath the Big Dipper and the northern lights dancing on the rim of the world, beneath the watchful eye of the moon, her grandfather's spirit left him and rose from the belly of the sled he had built with his own two hands, flew above his worried granddaughter, above the racing dogs, above treetops lining the river, above the hills, toward beckoning white mountains towering in the distance.

The spirit of Sampson Yazzie soared above the world like a raven.

7

Hwtiitł
Potlatch

Two days after Sampson died the small village church was packed for his memorial service. Delia and all four of her siblings, a brother and three sisters, were there, seated in the first pew. It was the first time in years that they had all come together. Death is like that, tearing lives apart while at the same time bringing lives together. It seemed as if everyone who ever knew Sampson was in attendance. Even Sampson's cousin Joseph came on his snowmobile. Denny's father was also there, though he never said a word to his daughter, or even looked at her, for that matter.

After the congregation sang several songs from a black hymn book, Denny scribbled a poem on the back of the funeral program.

Hymn Singer

At grandfather's funeral
I watch my father
mouth words to "Amazing Grace"

Tsin'aen ne'k'eltaeni
Tsin'aen ne'k'eltaeni
and I am a stranger
dressed in something black.

When she was done, Denny neatly folded the paper and shoved it into her coat pocket, planning to rewrite the poem into her diary when she got home.

At home that evening after the long church service, Denny's grandmother spoke without looking up from her sewing.

"U'eł txast'aas."

Delia looked at her daughter for translation.

"She says she wants to give Grandpa a potlatch."

"Okay, Mom," said Delia in English. "We'll give Dad a potlatch. I'll make some phone calls in the morning."

Although living things huddled or moved slowly during winter, word of Sampson's potlatch traveled quickly. Three days after he died, the whole village held a potlatch in the community hall. It was -35 degrees that afternoon. Everyone from the village was there, as well as over a hundred people from other villages who braved the cold to be part of the celebration. It's an important thing when an elder dies. Two men who were related to Sampson went out and shot a cow moose, as was customary to feed all the potlatch guests, which are called *dzoogaey*. Although it was not hunting season, the government allowed a moose or caribou to be harvested for a potlatch—perhaps the single most important cultural tradition still remaining in the villages.

It was the duty of kin to prepare for the potlatch.

Women spent the day before cooking enough food for all the *dzoogaey* and filling boxes with dry goods and gathering blankets to be given away at the potlatch. The more respected the deceased, the more blankets.

Men took turns hacking a grave in the frozen earth. Because the earth was frozen many feet below the surface, they built a series of fires—one atop the other—each of them allowed the diggers to pierce the concrete-hard earth a few more inches. They repeated the painstaking process until the hole was deep enough to bury the dead. It was as much an honor to dig the grave as it was to be a pall bearer at the funeral. Families also pulled brand new rifles from their closets, still in boxes. Potlatch rifles were rarely used for hunting. Instead, they were a measure of wealth to be shared. If the men felt they didn't have enough rifles, they went out and bought more from other men or from the local store, which always kept a good supply on hand for such events. It was customary to bring high-powered hunting rifles, especially lever-actions, like in the old westerns. As with the blankets, the more respected the departed, the more the number of rifles.

Denny also wanted to honor her grandfather with a rifle. But because she was too young to buy one from the store legally, she gave her mother $300 from her winnings to buy a gun for her grandfather.

Younger people, teenagers mostly, helped to sweep the community hall, shovel snow from around the doors, and set up all the folding chairs and tables. They also helped carry in all the food and blankets and guns when it was time. Everyone seemed to have a role to play.

As Sampson's widow, it fell to Denny's grandmother to perform the role of host of the potlatch. Naturally, Denny and her mother helped to make all the necessary arrangements, as did others in the village, though everyone understood his or her role. Denny and her mother also helped cook pots and pots of food, which they placed outside on the cabin porch until it was time.

"Denny," said her grandmother, "go out to the shed and load all the potlatch blankets into the truck." Only she used the Indian word for the blankets, which is *hwtiitł ts'ede'*.

Denny put on her parka and hat and gloves and went outside. Thinking it was time to go for a run, the dogs started jumping and barking and howling.

"Not today!" she yelled above the din. "Settle down! Settle!"

The dogs quieted, most whining as they paced excitedly on their short chains.

Denny walked up to Kilana, and knelt to pet him.

"Grandpa's gone," she said, wrapping her arms around the dog's shaggy head and hugging him. She began to cry on hearing the words spoken aloud.

The dog licked her face.

After standing and wiping her eyes, Denny opened the shed door and stared at the stacks of colorful blankets, all still in their clear plastic bags.

There must be a hundred blankets here, she thought.

Carrying five or six at a time, she made almost twenty trips from the shed to load them all into the back of the pick-up truck. The dogs watched her from inside their little straw-filled houses, hopeful that she might go to the sled at any moment, though even they knew it was far too cold for running the trail.

That afternoon, after loading all the pots of food between the blankets so that they wouldn't tip over, and after stacking nine rifles behind the driver's seat, all that her mother and grandmother could find in the house, Denny and her mother drove to the community hall and unloaded all the gifts and food.

Silas Charley and his older sister, Valerie, had come early to help set up the folding chairs and tables. Valerie had graduated high school three years earlier and was a cashier at the only store in the village. She was even more shy and withdrawn than her brother. When Silas had finished setting up the chairs, he helped Denny carry in the food for the potlatch.

"Do you want me to bring in the blankets now, Ms. Yazzie?" he asked Delia when all the boxes had been brought into the kitchen.

"Not until after we eat," Denny's mother replied with a thankful smile. "It's not going to hurt them to stay outside until then."

By five o'clock, all the food had been delivered and all the guests had arrived. Many had come from neighboring villages up and down the river. Hundreds of people sat in two rows of metal chairs—one row along the wall facing toward the middle of the room and one row facing them, with several feet in between, leaving space for later events. Two girls carrying a large roll of white paper walked down the middle of the rows, pulling a long sheet of paper from the roll and setting it on the floor like a giant placemat. Elders smiled at the girls. The entire room was filled with conversations. A few of the oldest elders spoke among themselves in their native language.

The rest spoke in English.

When it was time, younger people began to carry the food down the rows, the guests filling their plates with traditional foods like moose soup and salmon-head soup and smoked salmon, among many others. Denny carried two pots by their handles, one in each hand.

"Beaver or porcupine?" she said to most of the guests, asking which one they wanted.

To the elders, she asked in the old language.

"Tsa' 'eł nuuni?"

The word for porcupine always made her smile. It rhymed with the word for mouse.

Silas carried a big tray with chunks of boiled moose meat.

"This one tough old *deyaazi*," he overheard one elderly woman say after taking a bite. "It hard to chew."

Silas turned to Denny and asked what *deyaazi* meant.

"It means a cow moose," she said, knowing that her grandfather would have been proud that of all her generation no other young person knew the language the way she did.

Aside from the traditional foods, there were also pots of spaghetti, macaroni and cheese, coleslaw, baked beans, biscuits and rolls and fry bread, as well as dozens of cakes and pies and trays full of cookies. Through a special school program when she was in junior high school, Denny had been invited to participate at a potlatch in an Eskimo village up north. Added to the menu was whale blubber, walrus, seal, and Eskimo ice cream, a delicacy made of rendered whale fat with berries and sugar. At that potlatch, close family members wore the clothes of the dead as a way of temporarily reconnecting to their lost loved one.

Denny saw her schoolmates leaning against a back wall, listening to music through headphones, tuning out everything around them, while two eighth-graders walked around with kettles of hot tea.

"*Tsaey?*" they had been instructed to ask in Indian, though the word was actually Russian, from a bygone era when Russia had owned the land. Maybe a hundred words in their language came from that time, mostly the names of dry goods.

When the community meal was over, all the paper plates and plasticware were thrown away, the giant paper floor mat removed, and the floor swept or mopped where there was a mess or spilled tea. Only after the great hall was cleaned did Denny's grandmother give the signal to begin the potlatch. All the chairs on the outside—those facing the wall—were turned around so that everyone could look into the middle of the room. Silas Charley helped two boys to spread out large blue tarps across the floor.

For the next half hour, dozens of people carried in the potlatch gifts from cars parked outside and stacked them on the tarps. They brought in blankets, boxes of food or clothing, rifles, and envelopes containing cash, which they handed to Denny's grandmother. The pile grew larger and larger, a sure sign that Sampson had been well-respected. Everything was ice-cold from sitting in parked vehicles outside during the long supper. At -38, the metal on the guns could burn exposed hands and fingers. Once inside, the black metal of the rifles turned gray with frost. As the gifts were brought in, each family gave Denny's grandmother an accounting of the number of items they brought. It was Denny's job to catalog everything and add up all the numbers. Unbeknownst to her mother, Denny had brought her journal in which to write the figures as a keepsake.

When the last gift was set atop the mountainous pile, Denny's grandmother stepped forward to say the *hwtiitł kołdogh*, the potlatch speech. As was custom, she began by reading the list of all the gifts.

"One thousand six hundred and twelve blankets, seventy-two boxes of food, fourteen pairs of beaded moccasins, four pairs of sealskin gloves, two snowmobile helmets, two handmade parkas with wolf fur . . ." she read.

The audience listened, waiting to hear the number of rifles, always a measure of respect.

". . . two sets of pots and pans, one box of dishes . . ."

A little girl ran out across the floor, followed by her embarrassed mother, trying to catch her.

". . . two thousand one hundred and fifteen dollars cash . . ."

Everyone strained to hear the final number.

". . . and eighty-seven rifles."

Many of the elders leaned back and nodded. Eighty-seven was a good number. They had seen higher, but usually at a potlatch for a chief. Several elders recalled the potlatch for the chief of a neighboring village where over two hundred rifles were offered in respectful memory. It was said that the chief was 117 years old when he died.

Having read the list of gifts, Sampson's widow stood and, in her native language, thanked everyone for coming. She spoke briefly about how long they had been married and what a good man her husband had been. She talked about how much he loved his family and how much he loved the wilderness.

Denny and her mother wept as she spoke, though Delia, like most of the guests in the hall, didn't understand a single word she said. When the hostess was finished, she gave a similar speech in English, talking about how, when she was a little girl, potlatches used to go on for days and only in the summertime, when it was warm and they could be held outside in a big field. She talked about how there would be tents everywhere.

Once the speech was over, the handing out of the gifts began. Only members of the family could hand out the gifts to the guests, and gifts could only be given to people who were not related, particularly to those belonging to a different clan, which was determined by the mother's side. Because of this, Denny was *Tsisyu* clan, while her father was *Talcheena*. Knowing who was related to whom was very important. Indians introduce themselves based on kinship, the way some people introduce themselves with business cards.

"I'm so-and-so's cousin on his mother's side," someone might say.

"My father is such-and-such, who used to be your uncle when he was married to your mother's oldest sister," another might say.

It was the job of the host elder to tell what to give to whom. Denny and her mother awaited instructions.

"Give three blankets, one of them rifles, and fifty dollars to that man there," she said, pulling money from the thick envelope and pointing to the man sitting patiently, waiting to be recognized properly as a guest.

Denny gave the gifts to the man, who nodded and quietly said *tsin'aen*, thank you.

And so matters proceeded.

And although kinship is based on the mother's side of the

family, men and women are awarded gifts equally, women receiving rifles as well—though, in truth, not as often as men. Denny's grandmother also made sure to reward the young men who dug the grave, giving them each a rifle and some money. She also gave a rifle to each of the four pallbearers.

For almost two hours, the gifts were distributed in such a manner, until the floor was empty and almost everyone in the audience had a neat pile of gifts in front of him. Some of the elder men, especially the ones who would sing and drum later, had as many as three or four rifles.

In preparation for the dance, called the *hwtiitł c'edzes,* the blue tarps were folded up and put away, the floor hastily swept, and a string stretched about seven or eight feet high across the center of the room, over which were hung hundreds of colorful handkerchiefs. Several elder men with traditional skin drums, called *ghle-li,* took their special place and began to beat their drum and sing in their native language. And while most people danced, almost no one understood a word of any of the songs.

Denny sometimes worried what would happen to the potlatch when, in a matter of a few years, none of the elder men would be around to sing and drum. As far back as she could recall, women never sang or drummed. Who would take their place? Who would tell the old stories and teach the old ways? As the only young person who could speak the language, she wondered what her role would be in the uncertain future. For years, she had been writing down the words she learned from elders, hundreds of words, perhaps a thousand. Would they call on her to help carry on the language and customs? Or would they turn their backs on her because she was a blue-eyed half-breed with light-colored skin whose father didn't love her?

Already, some Indians wouldn't have anything to do with Denny, no matter how nice she was to them, like Alexie Senungutuk, who was almost the same age, but from a different tribe.

"We true skins ain't gonna have nothin' to do with someone like you, someone with an eyedropper-full of Indian blood!" he had once told her, his voice as vicious as a wolverine with its paw stuck in a steel trap. "We'll never accept you! You ain't nothin'!"

After that, Alexie did his best to convince other Indians to exclude Denny from everything. He tried to turn her into a cowering shadow for other Indians to stomp on. For the most part, it worked. Denny learned the hard way that whoever said words can't hurt was wrong. Alexie wielded his tongue like a switchblade that he flicked open to cut anyone in his way, and his sharp-edged words left scars.

The rejection Denny felt was like a hole in her chest big enough for a moose to step through. Lots of people are like Alexie—figuring the only way they can elevate their standing in society is by destroying others, even in such a small, closed group. Truth be told, Alexie wasn't full-blood either, but he liked to think he was. He liked to think he knew everything and spoke for all Indians. But he didn't. He was a big bully who didn't even speak his grandmother's language or hunt and fish like other men.

He had never caught a salmon in his life.

The summer before he and Denny were to start high school, Alexie drowned when his uncle's boat capsized on the river.

But the scars he left never went away.

With a handkerchief in each hand, Denny danced the way her grandfather had taught her, stomping the floor hard, the way boys and men did.

"You have to stomp so hard that the floor shakes," she remembered him once telling her. "If your feet don't hurt, you not doin' it right."

For over an hour Denny danced in the inner circle, where only boys and men usually danced. Girls and women usually formed a large slow-moving circle around the center. Out of the corner of her eye, Denny saw her father dancing his way toward her. For a long time, they danced side by side, each bent over, trying to stomp out all the hurt and grief inside. It was as if they were both trying to stomp the past into dust.

Finally, her father leaned in close.

"I'm sorry about your grandfather," he said just loud enough to be heard above the drums and singing and stomping. "He was a good man."

Still dancing, Denny nodded in a way that merely acknowledged that she had heard and agreed with his words.

But no matter how hard she tried to hold back her feelings, no matter how much she tried to redirect the hurt through dance, she couldn't control the emotions rising in her like a flooding river. Halfway through the song, she ran out the front door without her coat.

The temperature outside had fallen to -40 degrees.

Johnny Shaginoff, Norman Fury, and Mary Paniaq were standing in the shadows at the corner of the building sharing a near-empty bottle of liquor. None of them was wearing gloves or hats, despite the bitter cold.

"Hey, man," said Johnny, offering a drink to Denny. "I don't mean to disrespect your grandpa or nothin', but this party blows."

Then he had a coughing fit.

"Yeah," agreed Mary, snatching the bottle from Johnny and guzzling a mouthful. "This is boring."

Norman Fury took the bottle from Mary, held it up as if making a toast, and bleary-eyed, proclaimed, "Here's to the old man."

Without saying a word, Denny walked away from them, past the parked cars, past the green dumpster, past the stop sign at the end of the driveway, until she was standing alone in the freezing darkness. She looked up at the clear sky with the starry arms of the Milky Way spiraled above, wrapped both arms across her chest with each hand tucked under a warming armpit, and as she wept she told the stars how much she loved her grandfather and promised to remember everything he had taught her and to live her life much as he had done his—close to the land. In the biting cold, her tears froze on her cheeks like jewels.

Far off in the hills a wolf howled, his lonely call followed by a long, hard silence.

Sometime around midnight, though exhausted from the long, crushing day—while the wood stove slept with a warm bed of ashes in its belly, and while her mother and grandmother snored in the adjoining room—Denny turned on the little night light beside her bed to read *The Old Man and the Sea,* which her teacher had assigned to read over the vacation. In her imagination, Denny couldn't help but see her grandfather as the old man. She read for half an hour before putting the book away to write in her diary, stopping at times to wipe her eyes and steady her nerves.

Dear Nellie:
It felt like this day would never end. We had a potlatch for Grandpa. You should have seen all the people. I don't think we could have fit ten more bodies into the building. Mom and I handed out all the gifts, which made me feel proud. I think Grandpa would have liked it. My dad was there, or should I say the guy-who-knocked-up-my-mom was there. For the first time I can remember, he actually talked to me. He said he was sorry about Grandpa. I'm still trying to figure out how I feel about that. Grandpa was a thousand times more a father to me. At the potlatch, I promised to try to live my life the way he taught me. I miss him already. I feel alone. Who's going to teach me now? I was going to write this poem in the morning after a good night's sleep, but I'm afraid I'll forget it by then, so here it is.
Yours,
Denny

p.s. I know poems aren't supposed to rhyme nowadays, but it's only at the very end. Maybe that's okay.

Potlatch

All day long guests arrive in our village
huddled along the frozen river
to mourn Grandfather's death.
From the sacred circle of our clan
skin drums echo and elders sing:

'Syuu' nac'ełtsiin yen
"A potlatch is made for him."

Pulses quicken to the rhythm
dancers stream like vibrations
across the wooden floor
heavy with rifles and blankets.

'Unggadi kanada'yaet yen ne'et dakozet
A potlatch song is sung for him in heaven.

Tonight I have learned there is an end
to everything, to every light
where even the falling of brittle leaves
breaks the solitude of night.

8

‘Ałts'eni na'aaye'
January

On her way home from school three days after Christmas vacation ended, Denny saw a white truck parked in the driveway to her house, the chained dogs in the yard barking furiously. Lincoln Lincoln was trying to load her sled into the back of his truck. Kilana was standing on the bench seat, trying to wriggle his head out the window, which was partially rolled down.

"What are doing?" she demanded, when she got to the truck.

Lincoln sat the back of the sled on the ground.

"Your mother sold me the dog and this sled," he said. "Sorry about your grandfather. I heard you did pretty good in the race, but your mother said she didn't need the sled no more, so I bought it for a hundred bucks."

Denny dropped her backpack full of school books and mustered all her menace.

"You can't take the sled! It's mine!"

"Like I said, I already gave your mom the money for it," replied Lincoln, lifting the back of the sled again and trying to shove it into the truck bed.

Denny balled her hands into fists, wanting to flail out at Lincoln with both hands. Instead, she grabbed the sled and pulled it back-ward, wrestling with the man who was bigger and stronger. They pulled at the sled in a kind of tug-o-war. Denny was losing.

"Wait right here!" she finally yelled and then ran into the house, bursting through the door.

Her mother was washing dishes.

"You have no right!" yelled Denny.

"Calm down," said her mother. "Let me explain."

But Denny wouldn't listen.

"There's nothing to explain. How could you?"

"Listen," said Delia, "we need the money. I have bills to pay. Lincoln paid a lot for that dog, and he offered a hundred bucks for the old, beat up sled."

"But it's not yours to sell!" cried Denny. "It's mine."

"What do you mean?"

"Grandpa *gave* me the sled."

"But it's too late now, Honey. I've already sold it. I have to sell *all* the dogs. I can't afford to feed them. Besides, it's time you got that sledding nonsense out of your head."

Denny heard the truck bed gate close. She ran outside. Lincoln was just climbing into the cab, roughly shoving Kilana aside.

Denny grabbed the man by the arm and pulled him from the blue seat.

"What the hell are you doing?" shouted Lincoln, breaking free.

Denny began crying.

"You can't have the sled. It's mine!" she sobbed.

Her mother came out.

"Denny!" she exclaimed, trying to pull her daughter away. "It's too late. Let it go."

"Wait one minute," she pleaded with Lincoln before running into the house again.

Moments later, she came out with a handful of money, mostly fives and tens.

"Here's a hundred dollars," she said pressing the money into the man's hands. "It's all I have left from the money I won. Take it! The sled wasn't my mother's to sell. It's mine. My grandfather gave it to me. You can have the money. Just leave the sled!"

Lincoln eventually agreed to return the sled, but he kept the dog.

As the truck drove away, Denny pushed the sled to where she always kept it and put it back on the wood blocks, while her mother watched with her arms crossed, shaking her head in disbelief.

Afterward, Denny sat at the small kitchen table by the small window looking at the sled and the seven remaining dogs and thinking about what her mother had said about having to sell them.

How can I race without dogs? How can I afford to keep them all?

She sat for a long time, trying to read *The Old Man and the Sea*, but she couldn't keep her mind on the book. Her thoughts always fluttered back to the dogs and the sled, the way flocks of small birds suddenly reel and turn back in the same direction.

Finally, the answer came to her.

She would enter the Great Race, one of the last great races on earth, a punishing race that pits man and dog against some of the roughest landscape on the planet. The prize money for any team finishing in the top ten would be enough to support her family for a year; maybe longer. The prize money for a top three finish could support them for years.

Denny told her mother the idea, knowing it would be a hard sell. Her mother listened with her mouth agape the whole time.

"But, Mom, if I place high enough, I can pay to feed the dogs with my *own* money," she pleaded.

"But, Deneena, dear, that race is for grown-ups. Only the best athletes enter. You're a 16-year-old-kid, for god's sake."

"But what if I win?"

"Denny, I need money to pay our bills *now*. I don't have enough to feed all those dogs," she said, looking out the window at the dogs sitting in or on their dog houses. "What if you don't win? What happens then?"

Despite Delia's arguments, Denny eventually convinced her mother to give her a couple months, until after the race in early March. In the meanwhile, she promised to earn enough money doing odds jobs to pay for dog food. Besides, there was still quite a lot of dried salmon in the shed.

Excited by the notion of running the race—the longest and toughest in the world—Denny called a couple of pilots who flew supplies into the village to find out how much it would cost to transport herself, the dogs, her sled, and other gear, as well as all the food required to feed the dogs for the duration of the race. The cost was well over a thousand dollars . . . *one way*! It would cost a little less coming home because the load would be lighter, the dogs having consumed all their food during the long race. But Denny didn't worry about the cost to come home. In her mind, she would place high enough among the finishers to earn the money to pay to bring her team back to the village. In her mind, all she had to do was get to the starting point.

But at that moment Denny had no money. She had spent it all on the rifle for her grandfather's potlatch and buying back the sled, which was hers in the first place. She sat on her bed thinking how she could raise the money she needed to enter the race.

Then she got an idea.

Denny gathered several empty coffee cans, rinsed them out, and cut a slit in each of the plastic lids. She made signs asking people to donate money to help pay for the transportation costs to be in the Great Race, and taped the signs around each can. The next day, after asking permission, she left the cans all over the village: at the general store, at the village tribal office, the school, the church, the tiny post office, the medical clinic that was only open two days a week, and at the community hall where elders played bingo on Fridays and Saturdays.

After a week, Denny went around checking the coffee cans. At the store, Valerie Charley stood behind the counter and watched as Denny picked up the can and shook it.

"Sounds pretty empty," she said, timid as an owl hoot.

Denny opened the lid and poured the contents onto the counter. Only a handful of coins spilled out, mostly nickels and dimes and a couple quarters. But there was also a tightly folded piece of paper. She opened it and read the misspelled note that had a penny taped to it:

Dog Sleding ain't for gurls!!

After reading the note, Denny handed it to Valerie, who also read it.

"I'm sorry, Den," she said, crumpling the note and tossing it into the garbage. "They're wrong. My brother said you done real good in that race. He said you almost came in second. I wish I could be more like you—fearless, ya' know?"

"What do you mean?"

"I wish I was brave enough to follow my dreams. Look at me. Look at this place," Valerie turned, gesturing at the cramped, near-empty shelves. "What future is there for me here? Am I supposed to be a cashier in this crummy store forever? I wanted to be a nurse, but I was too afraid to leave for college. I didn't do nothing after high school but stay right here and watch my dreams go downriver like ice during break-up. I'm terrified of failing."

Denny looked away when Val's eyes welled with tears. She offered some words of encouragement.

"My grandfather always told me that if you're always looking down because you're afraid of falling, you'll never see all the amazing opportunities in front of you. He also said that courage can be found at any time in life, at any age."

Valerie wiped her tears with the palms of her hands.

"Thanks."

Denny carefully scooped the coins into her hand and left the store to check the other coffee cans she had placed around the village. The can at the church was empty, the clear plastic lid lying on the floor. After checking the contents of the other cans, Denny had raised only $10.23. It hurt her that no one was helping, that no one cared.

Walking home in darkness, wondering what everyone must think of her and her dream, Denny passed a moose standing in a yard eating a willow. The moose looked at her with its big black eyes, still chewing.

Denny hurried past, walking on the other side of the road.

After doing her homework and taking a bath, Denny dove into bed and went to sleep without a second thought about her diary. But later, during the deep night, she awoke from a nightmare, gasping for air and drenched in sweat. In the dream she fell into the rushing river, the snatching current pulling her downstream. As she was swept along, choking and screaming for help, she saw everyone in the village standing along the shore, watching her, even her mother and father. She called to them, holding out her hand as she passed within easy reach. But no one extended a saving hand. Her father turned away. Finally, she was dragged beneath the surface where she saw Alexie Senungutuk wedged against a logjam, all decayed, with small fish nibbling at his putrid, white flesh. Suddenly, Alexie opened his one glazed eye and frantically worked his tongueless mouth, gulping like a fish suffocating on dry land.

Even underwater Denny could make out his garbled words.

"You ain't nothin'!"

Denny shoveled driveways and snow from the roofs of houses after school and on the weekends, convincing homeowners that the heavy midwinter snow might collapse their roofs if the weight wasn't removed. She even hauled firewood and helped to cut and split it. She didn't say a word to anyone about the reason why she was trying to earn money, having learned that few people in the village would support a girl trying to enter the most famous dog race in the world.

Denny worked tirelessly, until her back and arms were so sore that she could barely move. On average, she shoveled two roofs a day during the school week, three or four on Saturdays and Sundays, taking whatever people paid her. Some gave her fifteen or twenty dollars. Some gave her less or more. She was so exhausted each night that she rarely wrote in her diary, and she was so tired the next morning that she sometimes dozed off during class.

Silas helped her shovel three roofs one Saturday at the end of the month. Denny had promised to split the money with him. Silas said he needed the money to order a new pair of sneakers from the Sears catalog.

"You should see them," he said. "They're sweet! They're black and white high-tops that look like downhill ski boots. They're real futuristic-looking."

For half an hour the two shoveled waist-high snow from the roof. The work was more difficult the further they were from the edge, where they could easily push it over the side.

"This is hard work," Silas said, stopping to unzip his jacket and to admire Denny's strength. "Damn, this snow is heavy! How many of these have you done?"

Denny stopped shoveling. From the rooftop, she looked out across the village.

"Pretty much every roof in town," she said, admiring all the snowless roofs.

"How much money you made?"

"I have $963.18," she said without even needing a moment to think about it. "I need a little more."

"You know the exact amount? That's funny!"

Denny told Silas how more than just winning the race, she wanted to make her grandfather proud of her and that she wanted to be like him.

"I miss him," she said sadly, leaning against her shovel for a respite. "But when I'm out on the trail I feel like he's with me. You know what I mean?"

Silas nodded as if he understood the way she felt.

After that, the two friends went back to shoveling. At the end of the long, tiring day, Denny counted the money they had been paid and split it into two piles, holding out Silas' half for him to take.

"Now you can get those shoes you want."

Silas put both his hands in his pockets and shrugged his shoulders.

"You keep it. They don't have my size anyhow," he said, and he turned and started walking home.

9

Tezdlen Na'
Swift River

Although Denny worked hard to raise money for the race all through January and February, she also had to keep training the team, now without a strong leader. Three days a week, sometimes four, she ran the dogs. Between school and feeding the dogs, doing odd jobs, running the dogs, and doing her homework, Denny had no free time. But she remembered what her grandfather had told her.

Only things that are earned from hard work and sweat mean anything.

On a cloudy Sunday, with the temperature slightly above zero, Denny took the team out for a long day on the trail. She knew that racers sometimes cover as many as a seventy miles in a single day during the Great Race. She had to push her dogs further to prepare them for the hardship ahead, increasing their endurance. But she also knew that she had to keep up on her school work. She wanted to go to college one day. So she took *The Old Man and the Sea* with her, as well as her notebook. Ms. Stevens had assigned students an essay about the awesome power of nature, in preparation for discussing the novel.

Denny had asked if she could write a poem instead.

Twenty-eight miles down the trail, Denny stopped while there was still enough sunlight to read her book. She built a campfire beside a fallen log to warm water for the dogs' food, as well as to boil coffee and to keep herself warm. The ravenous dogs were utterly focused on their dishes when Denny saw a wolf peering at her from beneath the sweeping boughs of a large spruce tree not more than a dozen yards away.

The breeze was light, but the wolf was downwind and the dogs hadn't picked up his scent.

Anxiously, she looked for a weapon in the pile of wood beside the fire. She saw a club-sized stick about four feet long. She stood up slowly, shuffled close, and bent over to grab it without taking her eyes off the wolf. When she stood up with the stick in her hand, the curious wolf cocked its head and pricked its black and gray ears. With her free hand she tossed a few pieces of wood onto the flames and sat back down on the log with the stout stick lying across her lap.

The wolf also sat down, his black coat a stark contrast to the white of winter. He opened his long mouth in a yawn.

After a while, feeling that the wolf wasn't a threat, Denny spoke to it in a disarming, sing-song voice.

"What are you doing out here all by yourself?"

The wolf cocked its head again, even more than before.

"I've seen you before, haven't I?" she said. "Outside my cabin and on the trail the day my grandfather died. That was you, wasn't it?"

The wolf sniffed the air.

"You smell the smoked salmon, don't you?"

Denny reached into the food pack and pulled out a whole fillet of dried salmon. Without standing, she flung the salmon toward the wolf. It landed about five feet in front of the tree.

At first, the wolf didn't move. He sniffed the air again, raising his shaggy, black head high.

"Go on," encouraged Denny. "It's food. Eat."

The wolf stood up, stretched, and slunk out from beneath the concealing tree limbs. He smelled the fish, then carefully took it in his mouth and backed up into a depression around the tree's trunk. From where she sat on the log, Denny could see that the wolf's eyes were blue. From her grandfather, she had learned that all wolf pups are born with deep, murky blue eyes, but the eyes change to a golden color while they are still adolescents. Only rarely does an adult wolf retain its blue eyes.

"You have blue eyes just like me," she said. "Is that why you're alone, 'cause you don't fit in with a pack? I know how you feel."

With immense satisfaction, Denny watched as he ate the salmon.

A soft, quiet snow began to fall.

"Wasn't that good?" she said, when the wolf looked up after eating the last morsel, his keen eyes staring at her and then at the pack on the snow beside her, as if to say, *Another one, please.*

"Alright, one more, but that's all," she said, and she dug one more piece of fish from the pack and tossed it to the wolf, who, this time without any hesitation, gobbled it up.

Suddenly, one of the dogs saw the wolf and started barking, and then all seven were barking.

The wolf ran away.

After the dogs settled, Denny threw more wood onto the fire and took out her notebook from her pack. From her memory, she sketched the wolf peering out from beneath the tree. She struggled with his piercing blue eyes, but was more successful with his grayish-white ear. When she was done, Denny wrote a single word beneath the image and underlined it.

Tazlina.

It was the name of a nearby river, meaning *swift*.

While the dogs rested, and the low sun slid over the edge of the world, a few stars began to shine and Denny wrote the poem she had to turn in to the teacher the next day, the one about nature. She had been thinking about it all day. She held the notebook close to the fire to see. She figured that the other students would write about how dreadfully cruel nature can be, how powerful and terrifying. But Denny wrote her poem from a different angle, showing that nature can be beautiful and comforting.

"This Side of Midnight"

It is snowing again,
and the stars are silver as

candlesticks. It is like being
in a temple on some Far Eastern

mountain. In the rocking wind
and unshackled darkness

where wild rivers run,
this sunset is the color of salmon

breaching. Stirring the campfire
with a stick, I lack nothing.

A little later thereafter the temperature fell below zero, and snow began to fall harder, swirling on the wind. Denny was again standing at the back of the sled, squinting through the tightly drawn hood of her parka, the seven dogs pulling her homeward through darkness along the frozen river, a hook of pale moon at their back. Denny's headlamp illuminated the trail ahead.

Denny always thought that is was strange the way a headlight illuminates only a tiny, comforting circle in the vast darkness, as if the world ends beyond the circle, the world of a circle in which she was the perpetual center no matter how far she traveled, feeling as though nothing else existed in the whole world, ever.

It was a lonely, lonely feeling.

When she turned to look, the black wolf was following behind about half the length of a football field, his gait long and easy. He stayed there all the way, for twenty-eight miles, until he vanished into the forest when the small, yellowish lights of the village appeared around a bend.

That night, after eating leftovers from supper and taking a hot bath, Denny sat in the chair beside the wood stove reading *The Old Man and the Sea.* It was barely one hundred pages long, and she should have finished reading sooner, but she lingered on every page, imaging her grandfather as Santiago. She imagined Santiago with a granddaughter, teaching her the ways of the sea and of seafarers the way her grandfather had taught her the ways of the land. Was the sea Santiago's adversary or his friend? Giver or Taker? And did the old fisherman consider himself to be at home when he was on the sea the way her grandfather felt at home when he was in the wilderness?

In her mind, Denny decided that he did.

She also wondered if Santiago would have been content had he died out there on the horizonless sea. Wrenching a living from the sea seemed to give meaning to his life. In his heart, the old man knew who he was when he was out there alone in a small boat atop the great, rolling deep. The low sweeping clouds and the unfisting waves spoke to Santiago, the way the river and the wind spoke to Denny's grandfather.

It was the ancient language of the world.

After dog-earing a page to mark her place, Denny took out her notebook, worked on her sketch of the wolf for a few minutes, trying to get it just right, and then turned to a blank page to write a new diary entry before going to bed.

Dear Nellie,

I saw the wolf again today. He just seemed to magically appear at our campsite. I don't know how he ended up there. Perhaps he followed me. He certainly followed me all the way home! I don't know how to say this, but I get the feeling he's lonely. I think he was part of the pack that killed Ms. Holbert while she was out running. But I don't think he had anything to do with it. I think he was kicked out. Maybe that's why he follows me. I guess everyone wants a friend, even a wolf. I can understand that. I didn't tell Mother about him. She wouldn't understand. She'd just tell me that he's dangerous and warn me to stay away. I think Grandpa would have been totally amazed at how I just sat there talking to the wolf. I named him Tazlina; Taz for short. I hope I see him again.

Yours always,

Denny

Dear Nellie,

I saw the wolf again today. He seemed to magically appear at our campsite. I don't know how he ended up there. Perhaps he followed me. He certainly followed me all the way home! I don't know how to say this, but I get the feeling he's lonely. I think he was part of the pack that killed Ms. Holbert while she was out running. But I don't think he had anything to do with it. I think he was kicked out. Maybe that's why he follows me. I guess everyone wants a friend, even a wolf. I can understand that. I didn't tell Mother about him. She wouldn't understand. She'd just tell me that he's dangerous and warn me to stay away. I think Grandpa would have been totally amazed at how I just sat there talking to the wolf. I named him Tazlina; Taz for short.

I hope I see him again.

10

Gistaani na'aaye'
February

That Friday night there was a party at Mary's house. Of course, her parents were away, visiting relatives in another village. All the high school kids were there, even a couple from junior high. By eleven o'clock, only Denny, Mary, Norman, Johnny, and Silas remained. Like always, Mary was drinking, which was really making Denny angry. Silas was sitting on the couch watching a movie.

When Norman and Johnny stepped outside, Denny snatched the beer bottle from Mary's hand.

"Seriously! You have to stop drinking!" she snapped.

"What do you care?" asked Mary, reaching for the bottle.

"Because it's a human being. It deserves better than to have you screw up its life."

"I don't care about none of that. I don't want this baby."

Denny tried to swallow her anger. She knelt on the plywood floor and gently took Mary's head in her hands.

"Listen to me," she said, forcing Mary to look her in the eyes. "You can't change the way things are. I know how you got pregnant. I know who did it to you. Everyone knows. I know how frightened and alone you must feel. But this baby didn't do anything to anybody. It's not responsible. It just is. Drinking may make you forget how bad things are for a while, but it's destroying this baby. Every drink you take is erasing its future."

"Her," said Mary softly.

"What?" asked Denny.

"The baby," said Mary, running a hand over her belly. "She's a girl."

Mary started crying.

"I don't know what to do," she sobbed. "This baby is ruining my life."

Denny held Mary, who resisted at first.

"Your life isn't ruined," Denny whispered. "It's just beginning. I know you got a raw deal. Life isn't always easy, especially here in the village. Things don't always work out the way we want them to. But you can help this little girl to have a better life. You can give her all the love that you never got and teach her to make better choices in her life. She depends on you. She needs you. Don't ruin *her* life. This is a chance for both of you. If you . . ."

Just then, Norman Fury burst through the door in a panic.

"I think Johnny's dead!" he yelled. "You gotta do something!"

Denny and Silas ran outside.

Johnny was lying in the snow beside a knocked over garbage can and with a rag clutched in his fist. A red one-gallon gas can with the cap off was nearby. Johnny was still and his lips were blue. Denny unzipped his jacket and listened for a heartbeat and breathing.

"He's not breathing! Go get help!" she shouted at Norman, who was just standing there. "Go! Hurry!"

Norman ran off down the street, dogs barking at him, the tops of trees swaying in the wind coming off the river.

Denny began CPR. She had taken a short course at school one summer, and she remembered the basics. She squeezed Johnny's nostrils shut while breathing into his mouth in long, drawn breaths.

"Get down here and help me," she said to Silas.

"What do you want me to do?"

"Put one hand on his chest, right here," she said quickly pointing at the place, "and then put your other hand on top of it and push kind of sharp and hard every four or five seconds."

For several minutes Denny and Silas worked together in the tight illuminated sphere of the porch light, until the village EMT arrived to take over.

"He's breathing," he said, after listening for a sign of life.

Johnny's lips slowly returned to their normal pink, and he opened his eyes.

"What . . . what happened?" he asked in a daze.

"You were huffing gasoline, you stupid moron," said Silas. "You were pretty much dead."

Everyone knew that huffing was a big problem in every village. While alcohol and weed was hard to come by, gasoline was readily available, used in outboards, snowmobiles, four-wheelers, generators, and chainsaws. Kids, sometimes as young as ten or eleven, would pour gas onto a rag and hold it to their face, breathing in deeply to get high. But gas fumes are deadly, and many young people had died in the villages, some the first time they huffed. You could sometimes tell who was huffing by their chronic cough from the damage to their lungs.

"I'm freezing," said Johnny.

Silas and Norman helped Johnny to his feet and guided him back into the house and sat him on a chair near the wood stove. Denny put a blanket over him. The village EMT stayed for a while to keep an eye on Johnny, checking his vitals every ten minutes and giving him some pills for his massive headache.

"Your vitals seem okay, but you need to cut that crap out," he said sternly. "I'm not joking, Johnny. The next time could kill you."

"Big deal," replied Johnny, throwing his head back to swallow the pills.

Late Sunday morning, Denny hooked up the dogs and headed into the wild. She could feel the difference without Kilana; the loss of the one dog robbed the sled of a little power and speed. She felt it most when the team pulled the sled up into the hills. It was like having an eight-cylinder truck that ran on only seven. She wondered how well she would do in the race without a strong eighth dog as a leader.

Barely a couple miles out of the village, Denny turned around and saw the black wolf following the sled as he had done before.

She smiled.

For many miles, the extraordinary band of dogs, wolf, and girl made their way up into a narrow valley, flushing a large flock of ptarmigan on the way. Finally, at the edge of the tree line, Denny called for the team to stop. It took her longer to unhook the team without her grandfather's help. As usual, she built a fire to warm the water for their dry food. The wolf sat beside a nearby tree, watching her as she labored to feed the dogs. The dogs paid the wolf no notice, which seemed amazing to her.

When she was done, Denny spoke to the wolf.

"Hello again. We haven't been properly introduced," she said in a disarming tone. "My name is Deneena. But most people call me Denny for short."

The wolf swiveled his shaggy head.

"Your name is Tazlina. It means swift. I'm gonna call you Taz for short."

The wolf licked his lips.

"I know, I know. You're hungry, aren't you? Hold your horses. I'm going to try something, and you have to promise to be nice."

The wolf blinked and licked his lips again.

Denny had brought some old moose meat. It was freezer-burned but not spoiled. Before leaving home, she had thawed a roast of it, trimmed the ruined edges, and cut the roast into chunks. She took off her gloves, opened the plastic baggie, and pulled out one piece, holding it up so the wolf could see it.

Tazlina stood up, his blue eyes riveted on the meat.

"You want this?" Denny asked, and she tossed the chunk pretty close to the wolf, which gobbled it up. She threw another piece, but not as far, making the wolf take a couple steps forward to retrieve it.

"That's a good boy," she said each time he looked up after eating a piece.

Denny tossed each succeeding piece so that it fell closer and closer to where she sat. And each time the wolf fetched the meat, she praised him. With every piece closing the gap between them, the wolf became more unsure and nervous, pacing to and fro. But his belly urged him to come ever closer to her, until finally he was so close that Denny held out a piece as far as she could reach, and the wary wolf crept forward and gently took it from her hand and ate it.

"You're a very nice wolf,' she said, taking the last little piece of moose meat from the bag. "I'm afraid this is the last one."

Taz cocked his head and licked his lips.

"You have to *earn* this one," she said, as she sat the piece of meat on her knee.

Tazlina stood for a minute, glancing at the meat and then at her. A squirrel chattered in a nearby tree, and the wolf turned his head sharply. Seeing that it was only a squirrel, he turned his gaze back to the meat lying on Denny's knee. He took the last step with glacial deliberation. With one eye on her face, he took the piece. With one hand, Denny gently brushed the top of the wolf's head, her fingers gliding over his black fur and along his grayish ear.

Tazlina took a quick step back, staring into her eyes, unflinching.

"I didn't mean to frighten you," she said. "Thank you for not biting me or anything."

The wolf walked back to the tree, where he turned in a circle twice, lay down, yawned, and watched as Denny got up to throw some wood on the fire and to pour herself a cup of piping-hot coffee.

The wolf followed on the way home.

To Denny, the hardest part of mushing came on arriving home after a long ride on the trail. Cold and tired as she would be, she would always want to go straight into the house to relax, warm up, and get something to eat. But she couldn't just leave the dogs hitched to the sled outside. Instead, she had to unhook each dog and tie him or her to the appropriate doghouse chain. She had to put away all the rigging, being careful not to tangle it. She had to put away the sled and her survival gear. Most importantly, she had to feed the hungry dogs who had burned all their energy running on the trail.

It was almost an hour after Delia first heard the dogs outside before Denny walked through the door, her eyelashes thick with frost.

"We already ate, but I'll bring you something to eat. Sit down," said Delia.

Denny took off her boots and parka and sat down at the table, rubbing her hands together to warm them.

Her mother brought her a cup of hot tea, a bowl of fish-head soup, and a plate with two pieces of pilot bread—a hard, round unleavened cracker popular in villages for its durability. While Denny was eating, Delia placed the newspaper beside the bowl, tapping her finger at a small story on the front page. Denny leaned over to read. The story was about her and included a photograph of her holding her trophy from the race she'd run.

Teen Rookie Enters Race

Sixteen-year-old Deneena Yazzie is the youngest con-
tender in this year's starting line-up of the greatest
race on Earth. Earlier this winter, Deneena placed
third in a regional race among a field of some of the
best mushers in the state, qualifying her for eligibil-
ity. Her grandfather, Sampson Yazzie, trained her
since she was 13. Tragically, Mr. Yazzie died on his
way home from the race. He was 76. Deneena plans
to use her grandfather's handmade sled. She works
after school every day to train her team and to raise
enough money to transport them to the race start.
This is certainly one to watch!

After supper, Denny cut out the story and taped it into her notebook, all the while wondering who had talked to the newspaper
reporter about her. When she was done, she closed the notebook
on her lap and looked at her mother and grandmother, both sitting on the couch quietly sewing.

The race is in less than a month, she thought. *Will I be ready by
then? Will my team be strong enough?*

Denny casually opened the notebook without looking. When
she looked down, it was open to the page she had sketched of the
wolf, his keen eyes staring into hers.

11

T'aede kae tikaani t'uuts'
The Girl with the Black Wolf

It seemed like everyone in the village had read that newspaper story about Denny. During English, Ms. Stevens enthusiastically announced her idea that the class could create a blog site about Denny on which they, and anyone who was interested, could track her progress during the race.

"Imagine," she said, "anyone in the world could go to our blog to read how Denny's doing and see any photos that we post. She could email us on the trail whenever she's at a village with Internet access to tell us any news and what she's thinking or feeling."

Everyone agreed it was a good idea. Besides, it beat using classroom time to learn about adverbs and prepositions. After using the entire period to discuss how to create the site and what should go on it, Ms. Stevens pulled out a digital camera from her desk drawer and handed it to Silas.

"During lunch, go with Denny to her house and take a picture of each dog. We'll post each one with its name. And make sure to take some close-ups."

Later, while Silas was taking the pictures, Denny went inside the house to get a photo of her grandfather.

"We'll scan this and put it on the site, too," she said, showing Silas the photograph.

Silas nodded.

"Let's get a picture of you hugging one of the dogs," he said.

After taking a couple pictures, Denny and Silas walked back to school.

"Are you nervous?" asked Silas, while they were walking past several ravens raiding a garbage can.

"About what?"

"The race, dummy. What else do you think I'm talking about?"

"Not really," replied Denny. "I know my grandpa's spirit will be with me."

"You mean his ghost?"

"No. Not like that," laughed Denny. "Here, in my *ciz'aani*—in my heart."

That afternoon, Denny nearly tripped over two large boxes when she walked through the door to her house after school.

"What's this?" she asked her mother.

"It's your grandfather's clothes. I convinced your grandma that it's time to get rid of them."

"Why'd you do that?" asked Denny.

"It was making her sad every time she opened her closet and saw his things hanging there."

Denny looked down at one of the boxes. Her grandfather's favorite flannel shirt was folded on top, the one he always wore when the two of them were out on the trail. He had been wearing it the day he died. Denny picked it up, held it to her face, and breathed in.

It smelled like her grandfather's aftershave and campfire smoke.

"What's Grandma gonna do with these?" she said looking at both boxes.

"We're going to donate them. I was just going to load them in the truck."

"I'm keeping this," said Denny, clutching the flannel shirt to her chest.

"It's a man's shirt."

"I don't care."

"It's too big for you."

"I don't care."

"Suit yourself," said her mother, realizing that she had no choice but to agree or get into a big argument.

While her mother and grandmother were delivering the boxes of clothes, Denny darned a small rip in the sleeve of her grandfather's shirt. She found his wristwatch in the pocket, left there by her grandfather since the last time he had worn the shirt. Though it was maybe fifty years old, it wasn't a particularly expensive watch. The black leather band was falling apart. She carefully pulled the stem and wound it, careful not to over-wind it. The second hand began to move.

She put it on.

It was hers now.

That weekend, Denny ran the dogs up to the small cabin in the hills, the one where she had first seen the wolf. As she had hoped, Tazlina emerged from the trees just outside of the village and followed her up the trail. When she arrived at the cabin, Denny ran a tether line between two trees and tied each dog to the line, spacing them, as always, far enough apart to avoid conflicts over food. Afterward, she went inside and built a fire in the stove. When she looked out the window, she could see the wolf lying in the snow near her tethered dogs.

None of the dogs was barking or growling at their natural enemy, having grown accustomed to his presence.

After warming water on the stove, Denny fed the dogs while Tazlina watched with great interest. He could smell their food. While the dogs ate, Denny made a special bowl just for Taz. To the dry dog food mixed with warm water, she added some leftovers from home, which included bits of bacon, and a couple chunks of caribou and beaver meat.

With the warm bowl in her hands, Denny slowly approached Taz, speaking softly.

"Are you hungry?" she asked. "I made this special, just for you."

Twice Tazlina stood and turned to flee. But both times he resisted the natural urge and stood his ground, his belly winning over his instincts.

When she was less than ten feet away, Denny reached into the bowl and gently tossed one of the chunks of meat to him. He quickly gobbled it.

By now all the dogs had finished eating and were watching the spectacle, pricking their ears when they saw the piece of meat in Denny's hand.

"Did you like that? Wasn't that good?"

Tazlina licked his lips, his eyes fixed on the stainless steel bowl in her hand.

Slowly, Denny took two more steps, until she was only about five feet from the wolf. She squatted, holding out the bowl in her hand and placing it on the ground.

But she didn't move away.

"If you want it, you'll have to come get it," she said, realizing the torment the wolf must be going through, torn between instinctive fear and hunger.

But finally, Tazlina inched his way on his belly to the bowl and ate, stopping at moments to look at her, their eyes locked. When he finished, Denny held out a piece of moose meat, which she had saved specially for this moment.

"Look what I have," she almost sang, holding the tantalizing piece of meat on the palm of her hand.

"Come get it," she said, shoving her hand toward him.

Tazlina whined and worked his mouth noiselessly, as if trying to tell her to give it to him. Ever so slowly, he stretched as far as he could without taking a step and gently took the food from her hand. Denny stood up slowly, and the wolf did not run away.

That night, before Denny went to bed, she heard a faint scratching sound at the door. Looking out the window, she saw Tazlina standing in the small square of light cast by the oil lamp on the table. She slowly opened the door just a crack, the light and warmth pouring into the cold and darkness outside.

She stepped back and waited.

The wolf stuck his head through the door, but came in no further.

Denny took the last bit of a biscuit she had been eating as a bedtime snack and set it in the middle of the floor, about eight or nine feet away from the door.

"You'll have to come inside if you want it," she said softly, while taking a seat at the table.

For several minutes Tazlina just stood in the doorway, but finally, he crept inside with his tail between his legs, a sign of uneasiness or submission. After eating the biscuit, he bravely explored the room, sniffing everything, even the wood stove.

"Hot," said Denny, as the wolf backed away, furrowing his eyebrows, and without burning his black nose.

Finally, Tazlina turned in a circle, curled up on the plywood floor, sighed, and closed his eyes.

Denny quietly closed the door, stoked the fire, adding a split log, and climbed up the ladder to sleep in the loft, leaving a lit candle on the small table below.

"Good night," she said, hanging her head over the edge and looking down.

Taz opened his eyes, looked up at her, sighed heavily, and went back to sleep.

Sometime during the night, as the fire burned down and the

cabin cooled, a noise awoke Denny. She crept from her sleeping bag and peered over the edge to see the wolf whimpering and twitching and kicking his legs in his sleep, as if he were having a nightmare.

The quiet dawn was shattered by a ruckus outside. The dogs were frantically yelping and barking unlike anything Denny had ever heard before. Taz was scratching at the door and whining excitedly.

Denny knew that something was terribly wrong.

She climbed down the ladder from the loft, jumping to the floor when she was halfway, and ran to the window to look outside. In the half-light of early morning, she saw a pack of wolves surrounding her dogs. Tied up as they were, the dogs were unable to run away or to defend themselves.

Denny grabbed her parka and the loaded rifle leaning against a wall. When she opened the door, Taz bolted toward the wolves, running straight for the alpha male, a large gray-and-white wolf, and crashing into him with so much force that he bowled over the larger wolf. But the alpha was quick to his feet and launched into Taz with all his fury. Both wolves moved as fast as lightning, bearing their long, white fangs, each trying to get hold of the other's neck.

The valley rang with terrible noise.

Both dogs and wolves anxiously awaited the outcome of the contest, the wolves wondering if they would have a new leader, the dogs wondering if they would be eaten by their wild cousins. Denny wondered if this was the same pack that had killed the schoolteacher, or if this was Taz's old pack and the alpha the leader who had expelled him, banishing him to his lonely existence.

It was soon apparent to Denny that Taz was losing.

Three times from the porch she raised the rifle to shoot the gray-and-white wolf, but she couldn't be sure that she wouldn't hit

Taz instead. Finally, convinced that the alpha might kill Taz, she aimed the rifle above their heads and fired two shots. Instantly, the pack ran into the trees.

After the dogs settled down and after Denny was certain that the wolves weren't returning, she helped Taz back into the warm cabin where she cleaned his wounds, which weren't all that bad considering the ferociousness of the fray. Taz licked her hand more than once as she cleaned his wounds. Afterward, Denny made a pot of coffee and shared a breakfast of caribou sausage and biscuits with him.

By late morning, Deneena emerged from the little log cabin with smoke billowing from its chimney. The hungry dogs all stood up and began to bark for their breakfast. Denny stood on the porch looking out over the white valley surrounded by mountains, the wind blowing her hair into her blue eyes, with one hand resting on the shoulders of the black wolf standing at her side.

12

Unen tah
On the Face of Things

With the race just weeks away, Deneena had to train Taz quickly. She did this in between school and homework, earning money, and running her team on the trail. Sometimes, she skipped school to give herself more time, calling in sick. The teachers knew what she was doing, but they said nothing because Denny was an excellent student with excellent marks. Besides, they were proud of her. Missing a day or two here and there wasn't going to affect her grades. They understood that things would return to normal after the race.

"Gee!" Denny would say clearly, using little bits of meat to teach the wolf that the word meant to go right.

"Haw!" she would say to teach him to go left.

After Taz mastered the basic commands, Denny added two more commands to his repertoire: "Come gee" and "Come haw," showing him to turn completely around right or left.

Little by little, Denny replaced the meat rewards with praise and petting. Taz was extremely intelligent, and he learned quickly. Sometimes, Denny swore she could see in his expression that he was trying to figure things out in his mind. The hardest part was harnessing him to the sled. Tazlina didn't like being manhandled or tied up. He hated his collar. At first he resisted so furiously— trying to wriggle free, especially when she would try to connect him to the tow line—that his behavior frightened her a little. But the wolf never once snapped at her or at the other dogs, all of whom seemed to accept him as one of them.

Sometimes, after school or on the weekends, Silas watched the training, standing at a safe distance, marveling at the extraordi- nary relationship between wolf and Denny. While Taz accepted Denny, allowing her to hug him and drag him into position on the line, he wasn't so trusting or friendly with other humans.

More than once, Taz growled when Silas came too near. At such times, Silas would back away while Denny chastised the wolf.

"Taz! No! Be nice."

Day after day, Denny taught Tazlina every command he needed to know as a lead dog. Most importantly, she taught him the word to go and the word to stop. She taught him that "Line out!" meant to pull just hard enough so that the dogs behind him could be hooked or unhooked from the main line. She even taught him that the word "Trail!" meant to move the rest of the team off the trail to allow another team to pass.

The process was neither easy nor even.

Once, while on the trail, Taz tore out after a moose he saw, leading the team off the main trail and entangling lines and dogs in the woods. It took Denny half an hour to straighten out the mess.

Some habits are hard to break, she thought.

With only days to spare before the Great Race, Denny allowed herself to hope that Tazlina had learned what he needed to know to lead the team. With his added strength and endurance, Denny could feel that the sled was faster than ever. Taz was the match, if maybe more, of Kilana. Perhaps, if she had had Taz as lead dog during the race before Christmas, she might have won first place instead of third. When she stopped for a break on the river, Denny wondered what her grandfather would think. Would he be happy that she had entered the race? Would he approve of her continued training and the new addition to her team?

She decided he'd be proud of her.

While sitting around campfires, Denny also thought about the wolf, wondering why he was alone. Her grandfather had told her that wolves always run in packs.

"Strength in numbers," he had said. "That the only way to kill a moose or caribou."

Her grandpa had said that only outcasts wandered alone and generally only until they found another pack to join. After much contemplation, Denny decided that Tazlina must have been kicked out of a pack for some reason.

Perhaps, she thought, *he had challenged the alpha male and lost.*

Denny didn't like to think that Tazlina might have been part of the pack that had killed the school teacher in the neighboring village, but the thought had crossed her mind. Judging from the way the wolf allowed her to become part of his life, Denny decided that he couldn't have hurt anyone. But there were moments when she questioned what she was doing, questioned her own safety.

Once, after taking a lunch break on the trail, Denny was collecting the empty dog dishes. She didn't notice that there was still a tiny bit of food left at the bottom of Taz's bowl. When she reached to take it, the wolf turned on her viciously, baring his fangs with his ears held flat against his head. Denny saw a terrible fierceness in his eyes, primal and untamable, like wildfire. She dropped the dish and backed away with one hand on her knife sheath, her whole body tense with fear, her mouth as dry as a sandbar. Taz licked the bowl clean and then sat down and waited, the savageness once again suppressed. But it took a while before

Denny could muster enough courage to approach him and take the dish.

She would later write in her journal, "Sometimes I'm terrified of him . . . of what he *could* do to me if I forget what he is even for a minute."

That night after supper, Denny walked over to Agnes Isaac's house. At 80 years old, Agnes lived alone in her small cabin ever since her husband died six years earlier. She was the only woman in the village who still practiced the ancient traditional custom of facial tattooing. In all of Alaska, very few Native women had facial tattoos, mostly the very old. Denny's own grandmother did not have one. In fact, aside from Agnes, no other woman within three villages up or down the river had one.

"I want *uyida' neltats'*," announced Denny in Indian when the old woman opened the door. "I can pay."

The old woman motioned for her to come inside the cabin.

"Close the door hard," she said. "Otherwise the cold creeps in."

While the old woman poured herself a cup of tea made from a local plant called Labrador tea, she asked, "So, you want a chin tattoo, eh? It not like getting one in the city nowadays, you know. I do it the old way."

Denny had never heard anyone describe the tattooing process used by the old women.

"How do you do it?"

Agnes sat down at her rickety table and sipped her hot tea.

"I gonna coat bear grease all over a piece of thread. Then I gonna put charcoal all over that thread and stitch your skin with it."

"Is it going to hurt?" Denny asked.

The old woman smiled. She was missing several teeth.

"It make even a tough man cry."

Denny cringed at the thought of the old woman shoving a sewing needle through her skin.

"What do you want?" asked Agnes.

"I already told you," said Denny. "I want it on my *uyida'*, on my chin, just like yours."

The old woman looked into the eyes of the 16-year-old girl, searching for something, a sign of strength, perhaps . . . or doubt.

"Okay. I think you ready. Bring me that box," she said, pointing at a cigar box on a bookshelf.

Denny fetched the colorful box.

Inside were thread, needles, a small vial of grayish bear grease, and another vial containing charcoal made from a special kind of wood. Denny watched nervously as Agnes coated a long piece of thread with grease and then worked the thread into a small mound of charcoal, making sure that the thread was thoroughly coated. Then she held a needle over a candle. When it had cooled, she asked Denny to help her thread the eye of the needle.

For the next fifteen minutes, Denny gripped the base of her wooden chair and grimaced as Agnes stitched three vertical lines into her chin, each about an inch long and evenly spaced close together. When each line had been sewn properly, the old woman cut the thread near the skin and began the next one, stopping only long enough to dab away blood with a clean rag.

"Leave those in for a week," said Agnes, putting away her tools when she was finished. "They gonna turn your skin black on the inside. It gonna itch like crazy, but don't scratch. I take them out when you come back."

Denny looked at her face in a mirror, bending close to the glass and touching her chin with a finger, feeling the thread beneath the raised skin.

She smiled.

"How much do I owe you?" she asked, reaching into a pocket for money.

"Nothing," replied Agnes. "You the only young person ever ask me to do this. It important part of who we are as women. Maybe someday you do it for another woman and keep it alive. I teach you how."

Denny promised she would learn.

When she returned home, her mother and grandmother were already asleep. Denny was glad for that. She knew that her mother would be mad about the tattoo, and she wanted to avoid an argument, at least for the time being.

That night, undoubtedly influenced by all her recent hard work training Tazlina, Denny had a vivid dream in which she was a wolf running with a pack of wolves. The dream seemed so real and it seemed to last for a long time. Entire seasons came and went. When she woke up in the middle of the night, disappointed that the dream was over, she wrote a poem about it in her journal, giving it a title only after completing it, fully aware that she was borrowing it from a far greater writer than she.

The Call of the Wild

Once, I was a wolf living among wolves
on the stunted backbone of tundra and forests
where we hunted moose and caribou all winter
in deep, drifted snow, without escape—
where only the deep silence of the north
listened as we howled at the moon
and ran the glacial earth until I awoke.

On some still nights I hear them waiting
above the rim of this valley,
calling to me from shadows
like a visitor who comes to my home
and knocks on the door with both fists.

"What the hell did you do to your face?" Delia screeched when she saw the tattoo in the morning.

For half an hour, Denny's mother, livid, berated her daughter, saying things like, "You've ruined your life! No one will ever take you seriously! You'll never get a job looking like that!" and, several times over, "What were you thinking?"

Denny's only defense was, "It's my life" and "You don't understand me at all," the universal hymn of misunderstood teens everywhere, to which her mother shouted the universal parental response.

"You look ridiculous!"

Finally, Denny's grandmother put down her sewing.

"What would you say to me?" she asked, defiantly.

"What?" Delia snapped, turning to look at her.

"If I had a tattoo like that on my face . . . would you say those things about me?"

"Don't be ridiculous, Mom," replied Delia, crossing her arms in defiance and tightening her jaw. "You wouldn't be caught dead with something so stupid on your face."

"I wanted one just like that when I was her age."

On hearing these words, Denny sat down on the sofa beside her grandmother and held her hand.

"What do you mean, Grandma?"

"Back when I was a little girl, all Indian women had a tattoo on their face. Some had many. It was a proud mark of beauty, a way of telling the world we had reached adulthood. My mother had one, as did my grandmother and all my aunts. I grew up waiting for the day I would get one, too."

Delia had never before heard any of this from her mother.

"You wanted a tattoo like that?" she asked, uncrossing her arms and loosening her jaw. "You never told me anything about that. Why didn't you get one?"

"When I was only ten, I was sent away to a school where they taught us Indian children that things like that, even our language and the potlatch, are silly and superstitious. They said our language was nonsense and babbling. Some teachers said it sounded like a dog barking. I remember the principal called it gobbledygook, whatever that means. I was locked up in the basement many times for speaking our language. Because I was at that school, I never got my face tattooed. None of us girls who went there ever got one. We all felt ashamed. I regret it all my life."

The old woman looked into her granddaughter's blue eyes and caressed her cheek with a wrinkled hand.

"I'm proud of you," she said.

They both began to weep.

"Thank you, Grandma," Denny said, hugging her grandmother, smelling wood smoke in her long, gray hair.

Delia stood watching the embrace from afar, the way people watch stars from billions and billions of miles away.

Ten minutes before she had to leave for school, Denny sat down at the table to write in her diary, while her mother was in the back room washing up.

Dear Nellie:

I got a tattoo last night. Agnes Isaac did it the old way. I knew Mother would have a cow, that's why I didn't ask her first. I was right. She always puts down everything about our heritage, like being Indian is something to be ashamed of. But Grandma stood up for me, which really surprised me. We've lost so much of our past; I just want to hold on to whatever's left. I wish Mom could see that. When the last of our old ways is gone, what will we be then? Who will we be? Doesn't anyone care? Change of subject. The race is in a few days. My team is ready. I have enough money for the flight and the food . . . but barely. I don't know how this is all going to end. I don't know how I'm going to get home. I don't even know where I'm going to stay the night before the race. Sometimes you have to follow your heart and believe in yourself

and in your dreams. When you risk nothing, you risk losing even more. Everyone thinks I'm so strong, but I'm not. I'm scared. Let's keep that a secret between us.
Denny

When she finished writing, Denny laid the notebook on her bed, meaning to hide it in its secret place before she left for school. But in her hurry to get ready, searching madly for her gloves, Denny forgot, and the journal sat propped against a pillow like a heart laid open for the whole world to read.

When Denny came home from school that afternoon, she found a white envelope stuck to the front door with a piece of gray duct tape, binder of the world. Her name was scrawled on the outside of the envelope. She pulled it from the door and opened it. Inside was one hundred dollars in cash with a handwritten note that read:

For hotel. Good luck!

There was nothing to indicate who had left the money.

Denny went inside the house, still pondering who it could have been. No one was home. On her bed was a new pair of mukluks and sealskin gloves. She picked them up, marveling at the craftsmanship. Both were very well made, with heavy, tight stitches and excellent pieces of fur. Denny recognized the stitching pattern as her mother's and grandmother's. She tried them on. The mukluks—made of black bear, caribou, and white rabbit fur—would fit perfectly over a couple pairs of thick, warm socks. The short-haired fur on the outside of the sealskin gloves was silvery-gray with black rings. The gloves were insulated on the inside, with a long leather strap connecting them so they couldn't be lost.

Then Denny noticed that she had left her diary on her pillow.

13

Nadosi kayax ce'e
City of Ants

Two days later, in the cold and cloudy weather around noon, Denny's mother drove her and her team up to the tiny airfield. The truck and trailer were loaded with dogs, sled, food, rigging, and a large duffel bag full of Denny's clothes and survival gear. Silas drove up on a snowmobile minutes before the plane landed.

"Heh," he said after turning off the engine.

"Heh back," replied Denny.

"I heard you was leaving."

"Yep. The race starts tomorrow."

"I got something for you."

Silas removed a glove and dug his hand into a pocket. He pulled out an object and handed it to her.

"It's a rock," said Denny, disappointed.

"Ah, but it's a special rock," replied Silas. "I got it from down by the river. Had to dig it out from the snow. This is to remind you of where you come from."

Denny rolled the small stone in her hand. It was worn smooth from eons of tumbling on the bottom of the silty river.

"Thanks," she said as she stuffed it into a small pocket on her parka.

Just then the plane arrived. After the pilot turned off the prop, Silas and her mother helped her load the plane while the pilot crouched in the cargo area acting as loadmaster, trying to determine how the weight should be distributed to keep the craft balanced and airworthy.

"Let's slide those bags of dog food a little forward," he said. "Strap down that sled so it won't shift in turbulence," he commanded a little later.

Getting Taz and the dogs into the plane was another story. There wasn't a lot of space for them, and they kept trying to jump out. But at last they were all in.

Eventually, satisfied with the payload, the pilot closed the cargo door and told Denny it was time to go. While he climbed into the pilot's seat, Denny turned to her mother.

"Thanks for helping me out, Mom. And thanks for the mukluks and gloves. They're beautiful."

"Stay warm and be safe," her mother replied, giving her a hug.

Then Denny walked over to Silas, standing beside the snowmobile.

"I'm glad you came," she said, punching him in the shoulder through his thick parka.

"That hurt."

He smiled, rubbing the place.

"You don't know how strong you are."

Like most Alaskans who live in one of the hundreds of remote villages, Denny had flown in small airplanes before. She skillfully climbed into the cockpit and closed the door, making sure it was latched properly. After the pilot motioned for Delia and Silas to move far away from the propeller, he shouted "Clear!" and pushed the starter button. The small red plane coughed several times and then roared to life, belching smoke for a few seconds. When he was satisfied with the reading on the gauges, especially the oil pressure, he steered the plane to the far end of the airstrip, turned it into the wind, and gunned the throttle. In no time at all the craft was airborne. As the plane noisily clambered toward the low cloud ceiling, Denny looked at her village from the side window. She could see the school, the little medical clinic, the one church, the cemetery on the hill. She even saw her own house and the little dog houses in the yard. From the air, the village in which she had lived all her life looked as small and insignificant as a sigh.

The city below sprawled between mountains on one side and the churning gray sea on all three others. More than a quarter million people lived in the tiny, crowded homes beneath her.

From so high up, Denny could see the main highways, the boulevards and streets; the slow-moving and congested traffic looked like ants, what her grandfather called *nadosi*. Astonished and even horrified by all the traffic—more automobiles than the largest herd of caribou she had ever seen—she created a new word to mean "ant roads."

"*Nadosi tene,*" she whispered, smiling at her cleverness.

Her grandfather had told her it was okay to invent new words. "Language always changing, always adding new words or taking away old ones," he once said by the flickering light of a campfire, sparks flying into the night like stars. "Languages are like rivers, never the same for long."

As the descending plane approached the mid-town airport, Denny stared at all the motion beneath her. The downtown area was roiling in the bumper-to-bumper traffic. The whole scene reminded her of streams of ants on the march, searching for food or returning it to the colony. Everything was in motion. Denny thought about all those lives below—coming and going, getting and spending, scrambling over one another in their desire to get ahead, measuring everything and everyone by what and how much they owned, living every day with the same indifference as the day before. She felt dizzy just thinking of all those people living out their days in such a cramped space.

She thought up a word to mean ant city.

"*Nadosi kayax ce'e*," she whispered, feeling the words form in her mouth.

And from her perspective, it truly was a city of ants.

After an almost perfect landing, a white van pulling a covered trailer arrived to take Denny to her hotel and to transport the team to a kennel for the night, where they could rest for the big race in the morning. The sled and all her gear would be stored in the locked trailer for the night. Denny had arranged for the logistics and accommodations using the Internet at school. She had planned for everything.

Except, of course, for how she was going to get home.

A hundred dollars wasn't enough for lodging at a nice hotel in the city, especially during the well-publicized race when visitors flock into the city to see the start. Denny's motel was on the edge of the downtown area, far from the nicer hotels where tourists paid exorbitant prices for a night's stay and dined at fine, clean restaurants. Denny's room was dreary and depressing and smelled of cigarettes, despite the posted "No Smoking" placard.

It's just for a night, she sighed, while looking out the smudged window facing the concrete wall of an industrial building not ten feet away.

After fiddling with the television for ten minutes, trying to get it to work, Denny decided to go for a walk and to find someplace to eat.

Though barely even dinner time, it was already dark outside. Two men standing beside a car with a door ajar were arguing in the parking lot near the poorly lit entrance. The car stereo was blasting a rap song into the night. Denny tried to look away as she passed.

"What you lookin' at?" one of the men growled.

"Nothing," Denny whispered while contemplating her shoes as she scurried by.

As she walked toward the downtown skyline, Denny passed men and women alike sleeping on the sidewalks, their bodies pressed up against buildings to escape some of the biting wind. Perched as it was at the edge of the sea, the city was almost always windy in late March and early April. Denny couldn't help but notice that most—if not all—of the homeless appeared to be from villages, come to the city in search of dreams or jobs, only to find the dreams and jobs were like snowflakes, melting away in their palms when they tried to grasp them. The dream was almost always out of reach. Age and gender didn't matter. Perseverance and work ethic didn't matter. With the city's broad back turned against them, and with their village a faraway and sometimes unwelcome memory, the cold and mean streets became their rootless home. Now, instead of wives or husbands or children, empty bottles of cheap whiskey lay beside the uncomfortable sleepers.

Even from her village, Denny had read newspaper accounts and heard stories about how police in the city often discover the rigid corpses of drunks and the homeless in the snow banks, especially during the coldest, darkest months.

The victims were almost always from villages.

Denny's grandfather had once taught her the Indian word for whiskey.

"*Kon' tuu.* It means 'firewater,' because it burns the mouth and throat going down."

But seeing the wretched men and women on the streets, sleeping off a binge or panhandling for change, Denny wondered if they call it *kon' tuu* because of all the lives and homes it burned to the ground.

While it was true that there were few jobs in most villages, at least no one was homeless. No one slept on the freezing streets or begged from passersby. Even the poorest in the community lived with relatives or in a cabin of their own at the edge of a village, surrounded not by the indifference of cold steel and glass and asphalt, but by the beauty of mountains and forests and pristine rivers created from melting glaciers high in alpine valleys.

Denny saw her grandfather and grandmother in the defeated faces of the street people. She even saw her own mother. She shuddered at the thought.

How could this happen? she questioned the hook of moon rising above the tallest building on the skyline. *Don't their families care about them? Why don't they just go home?*

The moon frowned silently.

Though it was a clear night, Denny couldn't see the stars through the lights of the city. She wondered what it must be like to live in a city and never really see the stars, never marvel at the cloudy, outstretched arm of the galaxy.

For almost an hour, she explored the streets and alleyways until she found an all-night diner. She had breakfast for dinner figuring it's pretty hard to screw up pancakes, ham, and eggs. Later, when she walked out the door, she couldn't remember if she should go left or right. She looked at the downtown skyline, but that didn't help. With no friendly stars to guide her, she decided to go right, thinking a storefront up the street looked familiar, but after wandering aimlessly for an hour, she was sure she was lost. She couldn't even ask for directions because she couldn't remember the name of her motel or the street it was on. The room key in her pocket didn't help because the white plastic tag only had a room number etched in black: 26.

She was utterly lost and afraid. In the darkness, the flashing neon lights, the shadows cast by buzzing street lamps, and the roving street people looked menacing. The used-up women selling themselves outside of bars frightened her the most.

"Hey, Honey!" one woman with too much make-up snapped at her. "This is *my* corner! Find your own place!"

One drunken man offered her a swig from the brown paper bag he clutched like a prayer.

The occasional sound of sirens didn't help.

The race was in the morning. Denny needed to find her hotel and get some sleep. She began to panic, feeling like she couldn't breathe. Her insides felt as if they were being squeezed.

It's ironic, she thought as she turned and walked briskly up a street going away from the downtown area. *City folks would feel the same way in the woods.*

Denny noticed a tall man walking behind her. He was wearing an old, green Army jacket with a dirty hat pulled low across his scraggy face. She thought perhaps he was following her, stalking her the way a fox stalks a rabbit. After two blocks, she decided to shake him, as they say. She turned into a dark alley and walked faster. Seconds later, the man rounded the corner and followed her into the alley. Denny increased her gait almost to a run, nervously looking over her shoulder several times, almost stumbling on the uneven asphalt. When she emerged onto a dimly lit street, she turned left. Moments later, to her alarm, the pursuer also turned left. He seemed to be walking faster, gaining ground on her. He had both hands in his pockets.

Denny was genuinely frightened.

Here she was, a teenage girl all alone in the big city. If she disappeared, no one would ever know what happened to her. She reached into her pockets for some kind of weapon and pulled out the motel key. It wasn't much, but the rough-cut edge could be effective as a weapon, especially against the soft flesh of a face. She gripped it so that her knuckles turned white. After another block, Denny passed a bar with loud music pouring out the glass door propped open by a chair.

To her great relief, the man went inside, and that was the last she saw of him.

Finally, Denny recognized some landmarks, a coffee house and a pawn shop into which she remembered peering through its darkened windows. She was on the right street. Five blocks later, she was standing in front of her cheap motel, still clutching the room key like a switchblade. Two men were standing close under a broken street light exchanging something, looking around them furtively. When they saw Denny watching, they turned and walked away.

She found room 26. After some struggling with the lock, she managed to get the door open. After fixing the night-latch chain, she breathed deeply, turned on the fluorescent overhead light, and sat on the edge of the too-soft bed. She thought she was going to cry but held it back. After another deep breath she undressed and took a hot shower. Afterward, she sat on the rickety chair at the rickety desk with the busted lamp and wrote two sentences in her diary.

Nellie:
I HATE the city! I can't wait to get out on the trail.
Denny

Exhausted, relieved to have found the motel and relaxed from the shower, Denny crawled into her bed and immediately fell into a fitful sleep, dreaming of a million ants crawling all over her.

14

Denny's yuuɫ tezyaa
Denny's Journey Begins

By midmorning of the following day, Denny and her team arrived at the race starting point. Aside from the dozens of teams entered in the race, many hundreds of spectators, perhaps thousands, wandered amongst the racers who were unloading their sleds and dogs and hooking the dogs up to the rigging. Several teams came from out of state, and a few from Canada and other northern countries. Barking and yelping filled the air. Local, national, and even some international news crews from television and newspapers busily interviewed racers.

Once each team was ready, officials made sure the required gear was onboard. Eleven hundred miles through the teeth of an Alaskan winter is a long way. Because of the inherent dangers, racers are required to carry specific survival gear on their sled. Failure to comply means disqualification.

Every team was also inspected by a veterinarian, who looked to see that each dog was healthy. In the old days, dogs were sometimes run to death from exhaustion. Over the years, rules developed to protect the dogs, a kind of doggie Bill of Rights. At strategic check points along the 1,100 mile route, veterinarians would again examine every dog. Many would be scratched from the race because of exhaustion or dehydration or injured paws, among other ailments. Since losing a dog or two during a long race was commonplace, many teams start off with as many as twelve to eighteen dogs on the main line.

Denny only had eight. She couldn't afford to lose a single dog.

As the youngest racer in the field, Denny received a lot of attention. One reporter took a bunch of photographs of her wearing her old-fashioned parka and mukluks as she handled her team, hooking them up to the main line, her handmade seal-skin gloves hanging from their strings.

"You look like one of them old black-and-white postcards," said the reporter while squatting to get a good angle on one picture. "I can just see the caption: Eskimo girl and sledge."

Denny didn't smile.

She wasn't Eskimo. She was Indian.

Behind her, crews from ESPN and the BBC were interviewing Jasper Stark, the three-time winner of the race and the favorite to win this year. Jasper had numerous big-time sponsors. Corporate logos adorned his expensive jacket and his shiny, red pickup truck, the way a race car is covered by logos.

"What's your prediction?" asked the reporter from the BBC, his British accent unmistakable.

"Well, there's a good base of snow. If the weather holds, I think a new record could be set," replied Jasper adjusting his sunglasses. "This is a tough field, but I'm pretty confident. I'll try to set the pace early on. We'll see. Should be a great race."

After chatting back and forth about issues having to do with weather and trail conditions, the reporter posed a question.

"There are a lot of good teams here from the villages. Do you expect a challenge from any of those contenders?"

"Well, I expect two or three of the Native teams will give it a go. But, frankly, I think my team is the most experienced in the field. As you know, we won two qualifying races earlier this season. And some engineering students at the university redesigned my sled. It's made of the most durable and lightest material available. She's fast. Like I said, I'm pretty confident."

Jasper smiled broadly as he spoke.

The reporter sensed an opening.

"Are you *overconfident*?" he asked, pushing the microphone at Jasper.

"It's not about confidence. It's about experience and trail knowledge, and no one knows this race course as well as I do. Like I said, I predict a new record will be set."

The reporter thanked Jasper and then turned to his cameraman and drew his finger across his neck, the signal for "cut." Then he saw Denny hooking Tazlina to the front of the line. She was wearing her grandfather's red flannel shirt.

"Let's interview the girl," he said to the cameraman.

"You're Deneena Yazzie, aren't you?"

Denny looked up from her work.

"Yes. That's me. But most people call me Denny."

"We're from the BBC. That's in England. Can we speak to you for a minute? Do you mind if we put you on camera?"

"Sure. That's okay with me," replied Denny. "Just let me finish hooking up my lead dog."

When she was ready, the cameraman gave the signal and the camera's little red light beamed like a laser.

"I'm here with Deneena Yazzie, the youngest racer in the field this year. How old are you, Ms. Yazzie?"

"I'm sixteen, but I'll turn seventeen in a few weeks."

"Good for you. Can you tell me about those lines on your chin?"

"They're tattoos made from bear grease and ash. They're part of my heritage," Denny replied proudly, holding up her chin so the cameraman could focus on them.

"That's a good-looking lead dog," stated the reporter. "What's his name?"

"His name is Tazlina. I call him Taz for short. He's a wolf," Denny said matter-of-factly.

"He's a . . . wolf?"

"Yep."

Both reporter and cameraman took a step back.

"He won't hurt you," said Denny.

The reporter collected himself.

"We just interviewed three-time champion Jasper Stark. Have you met Mr. Stark?"

Denny looked over at Jasper, standing beside his diesel pick-up truck—the one he had won last year in addition to the cash prize—signing autographs for two boys. She imagined that if she won first place she'd probably sell the truck, which was worth $50,000. She needed the money more than she needed a big, fancy truck like that in the village.

"Not yet, but I know who he is, and I'm a fan. He's great."

"Stark says he's confident in his team, in his equipment, and in himself. He says there's no one in the race this year who can challenge his team. What do you say to that?"

"Well," said Denny looking around at all the teams preparing for the start, "there sure are a lot of teams here, and some of them look really strong. My own team is pretty fast, thanks to Taz here."

The cameraman caught Denny patting the wolf on the head and scratching him behind his ears. The wolf made a low groaning sound.

"Stark seems to think conditions are right for the record to fall. I guess that means he would have to beat his own best time. Do you think he can do that?"

Denny thought for a moment before she answered.

"If anyone knows this race, it's Jasper Stark. But, this race is so long. How can anyone predict what will happen? You just never know."

"You heard it folks. It's anyone's race. Even a 16-year-old girl might win. On behalf of our millions of viewers around the world, I wish you and Taz the best of luck."

Denny beamed a genuine smile.

"Thank you," she said. "I'm just happy to be running the race. Can I say hello to everyone back home?"

"Go ahead," replied the reporter.

Denny waved at the camera. "Hey everyone!"

After thanking her for the interview and double-checking the spelling of her name, the reporter turned and walked away, remarking to his cameraman what a nice young woman she was.

By late morning, after all the gear was checked and the dogs examined, the race began. As always, the racers left the start gate separated by a few minutes to avoid piling up or bottlenecking on the narrow trail. As the reigning champion, Jasper Stark was first. Denny was twenty-seventh. The route had been mostly the same for decades, following rivers, through mountainous passes, past small villages of barely a dozen or so cabins, and finally along the sea as the racers made their way to the finish line. All racers were required to stop at more than two dozen check points and to overnight at certain places to ensure adequate rest for mushers and dogs alike. Eleven hundred miles is a long way to go.

Denny tried to put the distance into perspective.

Eleven hundred miles was three hundred miles longer than Alaska's length north to south. The length of the Alaska Pipeline was only eight hundred miles. It was like driving from upstate New York to Nashville, Tennessee or Ocala, Florida. In Europe, a train traveling eleven hundred miles would pass through the boundaries of numerous small nations and through populations of over a hundred million people.

The race record was a little over fifteen days.

Fifteen days! That meant a team had to cover roughly 75 miles a day. Denny had done the calculation long ago. She had never done anything like that in her training, because there wasn't enough time with everything else she had to do. She worried that she was in way over her head, that her team couldn't keep such a pace for so long a distance. But she swallowed her doubts and fears and prepared herself for what was ahead, remembering what her grandfather had told her about trying your best, even if you fail.

For the most part, the first day was uneventful. The field stayed pretty much in the order they left the gate. A few racers jockeyed to move closer to the leaders. Even Denny leapt into the top twenty. But this early in the race, with so many miles to go, no one was going to push his dogs too hard. As predicted, Jasper Stark set the pace, which was fast.

But late in the afternoon, Denny came upon a scene that illustrated the danger of the trail. A team had rounded a bend only to come face to face with a cow moose and her calf. Moose often followed the packed trails made by snowmobilers and mushers. Every winter, thousands of moose were killed by automobiles and trains as they followed the snowless highways and railroads.

With her ears back and her mane bristling, the protective mother had launched her angry, thousand-pound bulk into the line of dogs, kicking and stomping. In her fury, she killed one dog and severely injured two others before she and her calf dashed off the packed trail and into the safety of the woods. Such encounters were one of the many hazards along the trail.

When Denny arrived, another musher was helping the driver and had already called for help on his cell phone. He told Denny that a helicopter was on its way to transport the wounded dogs for medical help; both suffered from broken ribs and legs. With eleven uninjured dogs remaining, the musher was determined to continue the race.

Denny knew that at least one such incident occurred during each year's race.

Hopefully, thought Denny as she continued down the trail, *this would be the last.*

In the Great Race, mushers don't stop just because it gets dark outside. Instead, they push on through the darkness, guided by their headlamps, barely illuminating the trail ahead, the dogs dimly feeling the trail with their feet. Some clear nights the full moon is so bright that its light casts dark shadows from trees, staining the white snow. Though inexperienced, Denny knew her team. They had never run so far in a single day. Now, there would be days on end of such punishment. She wanted to pace them, keep them strong.

For now, rest and a hot meal was just what the doctor ordered.

Sometime around midnight, Denny stopped alongside a frozen river and made camp a dozen yards off the trail. She would allow herself and her team several hours of much-deserved sleep and a hot-cooked meal. Before dawn, which came late in winter, she would break camp and once again hit the trail. After feeding the team a steaming gruel of dry dog food in warm water, she gave each dog a fillet of dried salmon and then examined their paws for injury, carefully splaying each paw apart and checking in between the toes.

After the full-bellied dogs were bedded down for the night, Denny ate her own meal and afterwards cut spruce boughs for her bed. She stripped down to her long johns and crawled into her sleeping bag, still wearing her thick wool socks and a black wool cap. She cringed all the way because the inside of the sleeping bag was the same temperature as the outdoors, which was below zero. It took a few minutes for her body heat to warm up the ice-cold bag.

She was asleep only a few minutes later.

While she slept, snuggled inside her warm sleeping bag atop the scented pile—snoring from exhaustion—stars slid above tree-tops, the nearby river heaved and strained to turn over in its icy bed, and the campfire burned down to a heap of gray ashes as cold as the night.

Other teams passed in the quietude, the only sound the soft patter of paws on packed snow, the huffed panting of tired dogs, and the scraping glide of runners as the sleds passed in the darkness. Taz opened his eyes groggily and went back to sleep almost instantly.

In such a long race, timing was everything. Everyone had to rest sometime, dog and man alike. When they did, other teams gained ground. But even those same teams had to sleep sometime or other, at which time their lead would be lost. Knowing when to rest and when to push on was part of the strategy. Racers like Jasper Stark knew it well. He mapped out his rest stops systematically, with calculated precision—a few hours here, an overnight there. Many a leader had lost the race by miscalculating rest stops. Sometimes, driven too hard for too long, a team hit a brick wall of fatigue and could move no further. Thoroughly exhausted, the dogs required eight hours of rest to recharge. By then, other leaders might be nearing the finish line or, perhaps, had already crossed it.

15

Ghelaay nen'
High Country

The next morning, after building a campfire to heat water for the dogs' breakfast and for her oatmeal and tea, Denny walked out on the frozen river and gazed in the direction she would travel. From where she stood, she could see that the trail climbed into high country. She could see that the valley became narrow and steep, forbidding and treeless at such altitudes.

It took an hour to pack up camp, use a tree out of necessity, and rig up the team to the main line. The dogs whined and leaped with anticipation, especially Taz. Denny was surprised at their enthusiasm, given the long previous day. She herself was tired and sore all over. Her shoulders throbbed, and her hands hurt from gripping the handle so tightly for so many hours. But most of all, her lower back ached from standing on the back of the sled all day. She wished she could sit in the little sweathouse behind her cabin for a while to soothe her muscles.

It wasn't long before the team was in the mountain pass. To Denny's dismay, screeching winds funneled through the valley had scoured snow from the ground, exposing large and small rocks frozen to the earth as if they had been set in concrete. The going was rough on dog paws, rough on the sled, and rough on the driver. The constant jolting rattled Denny's teeth and her bones, and her arms felt as if they were being wrenched from their sockets.

After crossing a particularly treacherous stretch of exposed rock, Denny saw blood on the trail.

"Whoa!" she shouted. "Stop!"

Taz brought the team to an abrupt standstill. Denny tried to set the brake hook, but the ground was so frozen that the sharp hooks wouldn't penetrate. Instead, she tied a snub line around a boulder.

"See if you can move that," she said to the team after cinching the knot.

Methodically, from the front of the line to the back, Denny lifted each dog's paw to see which one was bleeding. It was one of the mid-line dogs, the one named Molly. She had thrown three of her booties, and one of her front paws had a cut from a sharp rock. Denny untied the dog from the tow line and guided her to the back of the sled where she treated the injury with a first-aid ointment. Then she bound the foot in gauze, and gently set the dog into the basket.

Molly didn't seem to mind.

"You can take a break until your paw heals," she said, patting the dog on the head.

Denny knew that such a minor cut would heal quickly, and the dog would rejoin the team by mid-afternoon. She'd make sure the Velcro straps on her booties were tighter this time. With her team temporarily weakened by the loss of one dog, she undid the snub line, put her gloves back on, pulled up her parka hood, and gripped the sled handle.

"Mush!" she shouted.

And once again the team was off.

As she rode along on the back of the sled, trying to keep from falling asleep from exhaustion, Denny marveled at the steep, rugged valley. The cliffs and crags looked as if nothing had changed since the beginning of time. She imagined dinosaurs roaming this valley long ago. But she knew better. Many times, sitting around a campfire, hot coffee mug clutched in both hands, her grandfather had spoken about the nature of Time and of Nature itself.

"Everything changes," she remembered him saying in his slow, deliberate way. "Forever and forever and forever nothing stays the same. The earth turns and each day the radiance of the sun spins into existence and is gone. Sea waves crash and scour the coast and the coastline changes. Rain erodes mountains, and rivers carry them back to the sea. People die and people are born. Glaciers grow and melt. Many are gone that existed when I was a boy. I have seen whole mountain slopes suddenly break free and crash like thunder into their valleys. They say even the sun itself will one day burn out. Nothing that comes stays for long. Live fully in *this* moment. Embrace that truth, Granddaughter, and live a happier life."

As young as she was, Denny already understood some of what her grandfather had told her. Year after year, she had marveled at how the river alongside her village changed channels, how sand and gravel islands appeared and disappeared, how tree-lined banks sometimes sloughed into the river, creating new banks. She recalled how most of the trees along one of her favorite fishing streams had been toppled in a storm, the creek bed and surrounding ground crisscrossed with felled trees and deadfalls, making it impossible to fish or even to walk through the once-forest. For over a hundred years the trees had grown there, and then one day the place no longer looked the same, nor would it for another hundred years.

Halfway through the pass, Denny came upon two teams stopped along the trail, the two mushers standing beside one of the sleds. One of the men was a foot taller than the other. Denny stopped to investigate, securing her team far enough away from the other teams to avoid dogfights.

"Any trouble?" she asked, as she walked up to the two men and pulled down her parka hood.

The taller man told how his sled had hit a large rock, which had overturned and thrown him, breaking his arm in the fall. The shorter musher had arrived about fifteen minutes later and helped to fashion a makeshift sling for the dangling arm.

"Are you going to scratch from the race?" Denny asked the injured man.

"I don't have no choice. I can't hold onto a sled with one hand for five hundred miles."

"Can you help me get him into his sled?" asked the shorter man. "I'll hook up his team in front of mine and take him to the next check point, which is about twenty miles away."

Denny knew that the reason he wanted the other team in front of his was because it was downhill all the way, and with the injured man resting in the basket, he would be unable to use the foot brake when the sled gained too much speed and they would crash into each other. In this way, the driver at the back of both teams could use his brakes as well as voice commands to control the descent. Denny helped load the injured racer into the basket, and then she tied a line between the teams.

"Does this look good?" she asked the other musher.

"It looks great," he said after checking the length and the knot. "You might as well go on ahead of us. We're going to take it slow. Tell the people at the check point that we're right behind you and that he'll need a doctor to set that arm."

Denny wished them both luck, untied her team, and took off down the trail, turning and waving goodbye as she passed. The whole way down the mountain, she worried something like that could happen to her. She knew that in the Last Frontier, it only took an instant for disaster to strike.

16

Son'de'aa
A Rising Star

Over the next four days, Denny pushed on toward the finish line. Unused to so much physical exertion for days on end with little sleep, both she and her team were exhausted. The white miles passed blindly at times, as if in a dreamlike trance. More than once she nodded off at the back of the sled, only to be awakened by some rough bump. There were times she even thought about quitting.

But at such moments, she thought about her grandfather and how he must be watching her, and the happy memories kept her going.

Little by little, relentless mile after relentless mile, Denny found herself in the top ten.

Hundreds of miles lay defeated behind her, but many hundreds of grueling miles lay ahead on the uncertain trail. Back home, unbeknownst to Denny, students at her school tracked her progress on a large map, posted blogs about her, made colorful pictures and posters they taped to classroom and hallway walls, read about her in the newspaper, and listened for her name on the news. In keeping with the spirit, middle school and high school students read Jack London's quintessential Alaskan adventure story, *The Call of the Wild*. Few teachers pointed out London's overt notions of su-premacy of the White Man over Indians—the steadfast mantra of imperialism and colonialism. America's westward expansion had been driven by it. For the most part, young readers simply liked a good dog story, and the story of Buck was among the best.

Silas posted the BBC interview on the school's website, editing it so that the reporter's last words played in a loop over and over again—"Even a 16-year-old girl might win"—each time Denny's beaming face popped up. At first, only a few hundred people vis-ited the blog site daily, not much for a website, but the numbers began to grow.

When Denny and her team pulled into one of the small villages for an overnight and to check in at the required veterinary station, several newspaper reporters from across the nation interviewed her. She talked about how her grandfather had taught her and how he had died while out on the trail with her. The next day, a photograph of a haggard-looking Denny hugging Taz adorned the front page of those papers. The accompanying story even talk-ed about the traditional tattoo on her face and how she was one of the youngest Indian women to have one and what it meant to her. Millions saw the picture and read the various captions: "An Un-likely Alliance," "Against All Odds," "Miracle on the Snow," and "A Mighty Underdog." Several of the stories hailed her team as the fastest in the field because no other team had gained so much time, surpassing seventeen other teams to make it into the top ten. Denny would later learn that one newspaper story hailed Taz as "Taz, the Spaz" because he had so much energy and was so fast.

Other newspapers soon adopted the witty epithet.

And while out on the trail Denny was oblivious to all the stories about her in newspapers and on television and websites, everyone back home in her village read the stories, even her father. Denny's mother proudly cut out every story she could find and saved them for her daughter in an old photo album. One of her favorites read:

The One to Watch

With an old-fashioned wooden sled handmade by her deceased grandfather and wearing a traditional parka, sealskin gloves, and mukluks made by her mother and grandmother, 16-year-old Alaska Native Deneena Yazzie is making headlines around the world, jumping from the middle of the pack to the leader board. While every other team has more than a dozen dogs—some with as many as eighteen on a double lead—Denny's team of eight, led by "Taz, the Spaz," is the fastest in this year's field. While it's too soon to call a winner, this determined teen is certainly one to watch.

After the newspaper and TV stories began coming out, the school's blog site got almost a hundred thousand hits a day from around the world. Despite Jasper Stark's ambitious prediction, the poor weather combined with a broken runner and two dropped dogs all but evaporated his dream of breaking his own record.

And Denny hadn't been without her own troubles. She had lost a little time when one of the lower stanchions on the sled broke after she hit a tree stump. Luckily, she was able to repair it temporarily with duct tape, one of the few tools she carried with her. Also, one of her dogs had succumbed to exhaustion and was being dragged by the others before she stopped and put the trembling animal into the basket to let it rest for six hours. A dog in the basket was common among racers. Some mushers regularly allowed each dog a brief respite in this way.

After a hot shower and a welcome dinner in the local school gym, courtesy of the villagers, almost every one of them Indian, Denny took a little time to email her own school as she had promised, telling everyone back home about the race and of her thoughts and feelings. She even downloaded some pictures from a digital camera one of her teachers had loaned her for the purpose.

One of her best pictures was taken from the back of the sled as the team raced along a frozen river, their breath rising like ice fog. All you could see in the photograph were tails and behinds of all eight members of the team—the barren, wintry landscape indistinct in the foreground.

There was a saying in mushing that said a lot about life in general: "When you're not the lead dog, the scenery never changes."

And while the respite of the village's hospitality was welcome, the trail beckoned. After several hours of deep sleep in her sleeping bag on the gym floor, Denny heard the trail's call and abruptly responded with thirty-two paws on snow.

Her mind wandered a great deal while she was out on the trail. While the race itself required a Herculean effort—more than a thousand torturous miles through one of the most remote and inhospitable landscapes on earth—the pace wasn't exactly blinding. Dogs pulling a sled heavy with gear, food, and musher don't move all that fast. The miles fall slowly but steady behind the sled. For the most part, the lead dog—or in this case the lead wolf—can follow the trail easily without much direction, awaiting a command only when a trail forks or the driver wants to stop to rest.

While there's little time for sleep on the trail, there's plenty of time for daydreaming and reflection.

During the monotonous hours, often as many as eighteen to twenty each day, Denny thought about many things: about school, about her mother, even about her invisible father. Mostly, she thought about her grandfather. Her mind kept returning to *The Old Man and the Sea*. While at first she had imagined her grandfather as Santiago, the tenacious old man fighting against all odds to wrestle the giant marlin from the sea, she now began to see herself in the role of a determined young woman pitting her strength and courage against Nature. As in the book, the natural world hurled itself against her and her team as they ascended mountain passes assailed by snow storms and by days and nights as cold as 30 degrees below zero. The wintry world tried to smother under snow and ice her dreams of winning, but, like Santiago, Denny persisted, driven by her pride—or fear. She wondered if the old man in the story was driven to challenge the sea by an enormous pride or by fear—the fear that he really was old and weak and useless.

If that were the case, she thought, *the story wasn't about Man against Nature at all, but about Man against Himself.*

In moments of such genuine self-reflection, Denny came to understand that a hero is someone who is also afraid but, unlike other people, hangs on for one more minute.

During her ruminations, Denny noted that she hadn't seen Jasper Stark even once. Because he started the race so much earlier than she did in the line-up, he was always leaving a village or checkpoint by the time she arrived hours later. But she had heard about his problems and his two dropped dogs. Judging on how many teams she had already passed, she knew he couldn't be too far ahead.

With that thought utmost in her mind, Denny put the pedal to the metal, as they say. On one clear night, she passed three teams ahead of her camped at the bottom of a steep mountain valley, confident that she could tackle the treacherous pass in the dark. If successful, her calculated move would push her into the top five. Sometime in the middle of the night, she was safely descending the other side of the pass.

From afar, the little light from her headlamp as she came down through the darkness must have looked like a falling star.

17

Hweł kuzyaa
The Storm Passes

Denny's gambit paid off. For the next three days her team stayed in the top five. Increasingly, media attention was focusing on Denny, who was becoming the Cinderella of one of the world's greatest races. If she won, said the stories in the newspapers and on television, she would make history as the youngest person ever to win the toughest race in the world. As more than one reporter put it, she was becoming "The Little Engine That Could." Back home, reporters swamped the village trying to get the scoop on her backstory. At the airstrip outside of the village, airplanes were coming and going almost hourly, bringing in reporters and magazine photographers from around the world.

Pictures of Denny's family's modest cabin with the dog houses out front appeared worldwide accompanied by stories likening her humble origins to the way Elvis grew up in a little shack of a house. By that time, the school's website was receiving hundreds of thousands of hits each day. The village tribal organization got the idea that with so much traffic, people should post advertisements of their handmade Native crafts.

Business was good.

People around the world ordered hand-sewn, beaded moccasins and gloves, fur-trimmed mukluks, parkas, objects carved from ivory or caribou bone, beaded necklaces, and carved dancing masks. Someone even got the bright idea to make T-shirts that read "Village Girls Rule!" and "Taz the Spaz!" He sold over a hundred in the first day alone. Everyone worked overtime to meet demand, realizing that when the race was over, so too would be the intense interest. Denny's mother and grandmother went into high gear, sewing and beading twelve hours a day. The school even created a scholarship page and received thousands of dollars in donations.

Silas latched onto the idea of charging visitors for rides to and from the airstrip, which was almost a mile away from the village. He borrowed Denny's mother's truck and paid her a percentage of the take. With no other means of transportation available, Silas's pockets soon bulged with cash. Without a single restaurant or café in the community to accommodate the visitors, some enterprising villagers set up hot coffee and sandwich stands, the way children in the lower states set up roadside lemonade stands on hot summer days.

Out on the trail, the weather worsened dramatically. With less than forty miles before Denny's team would emerge from the forest to cross a stretch of the frozen Bering Sea, a storm blew in across the icy Straits from Siberia. The powerful winds broke tree limbs and snapped trees in half, some of which fell across the trail, blocking passage. It got so bad that half the teams in the race stopped dead in their tracks, found whatever shelter they could find from the blast, and waited it out, in spite of the prospect of losing precious hours of time. The other half pressed on into the belly of the storm, Denny among them. The swirling snow, which seemed to blow in from every direction, even upward as if the earth itself was in a fury, was so blinding that Denny could barely see Taz at the front of the line.

But Denny pushed on through the whiteout until she came to

what was clearly a fork in the trail. Both paths lay equal before her, the wind and snow having erased any evidence of other teams that had gone before her and the markers knocked over or buried. She stood in front of Taz looking down both trails trying to decide which one to take, wondering what differing fate each held for her. The scene reminded her of one of her favorite poems.

"Right or left?" she asked the wolf, who looked up at her, squinting and blinking against the snow bullets blasting his eyes and sticking to his eyelashes.

Finally, she made her decision to go left.

As Denny mushed the team toward the left, she had no idea that three of the four teams ahead of her had chosen the righthand fork, the wrong direction. It would be hours before they realized the trail dead-ended at a lake nestled in a steep valley. It would take an equal number of hours to backtrack to the fork. Jasper Stark, in the lead, had chosen rightly because, when he arrived at the junction, the markers were still visible. But by the time the second-place team arrived at the same fork, everything was obscured. Only by chance, or by some innate sense, did Denny choose rightly the trail to the left.

Because the drifting snow was so deep and the howling wind so ferocious, the going was slow. Taz could barely distinguish the trail ahead from the surrounding woods. Open fields were the worst. With the trail buried under a blanket of undisturbed white, the wind sliding ribbons of snow snakelike across the surface, not even the wolf could decide where the trail picked up on the other side. Several times the team stopped while Denny trudged along the edge of a field looking for the trail. At one point she stopped for half an hour to let the dogs rest, giving each a large piece of dried salmon. The wind was too strong to build a fire to heat water for a proper meal.

Sometimes a half hour break is just enough.

While she rested, Denny wondered if she had, perhaps, taken

the wrong trail. She had seen no signs of the teams before her. But then she knew the drifting snow and the grinding wind would have eroded all evidence of their passing within minutes. She also knew that there were dozens of teams hot on her trail. It was only logical that some of them would choose the left trail at the fork.

Worried that other racers might pass her while she was resting, Denny examined each dog's paw for injury before getting back to work. She knew that an injured paw could spell the end of a dog's ability to stay in the race. Each dog had lost one or two of its booties. Taz had lost all four. Thrown booties are commonly found along dog-sledding trails. Like all mushers, Denny had a bag full of extras. As she put them on, making sure they were snug, she patted each dog on the head.

"Good job," she said.

She had a longer conversation with Taz, leaning close to tell him how proud she was of him.

"We wouldn't be here without you. You're so strong and so smart. If we win, it will be because of you. I couldn't have asked for a better leader. Thank you," she said above the din of the howling wind, pressing her face against his.

Taz's eyes were ablaze and never veered toward the surrounding wilderness from which he came into Denny's life. He snapped his jaws several times, his way of showing excitement, an eagerness to continue what must have seemed to him a curious but necessary goal.

Denny shuffled to the back of the sled, took her place on the small platform and, with one hand gripping the handle, deftly pulled the snow hook and shouted, "Let's go!"

Every furry member of the team strained against his harness, and with a jolt the sled with its exhausted driver once again set off down the trail.

Denny was too tired to pedal. Instead, she leaned against the handle trying to stay awake.

A little over an hour later, Denny came on a dreadful scene. As she broke through the forest into a clearing along a small river, she saw that Jasper Stark and his entire team had broken through the ice. Man, sled, and every dog had plunged into the icy water. The sled with its heavy load had sunk straight to the bottom, and even though the river wasn't very deep, the two dogs closest to the sled were dragged to the bottom, where they drowned. The rest of the dogs, fourteen in all since two of Jasper's dogs had been dropped earlier, were struggling to stay above water, climbing over one another pell-mell in their frantic attempt to escape the icy clutch of the river. Jasper was desperately trying to crawl out onto the unbroken ice, but each time he managed to haul himself partially out of the water, the thin ice broke beneath him. When he reemerged, his dogs would nearly drown him as they tried to climb onto his head. Denny had no idea how long they had been in the water, but she could see they were all exhausted.

Here was her chance to win the race. With Jasper preoccupied as he was, Denny could take the lead and cross the finish line sometime around midnight. She would take home the purse of nearly $100,000 and the brand-new diesel pickup truck, which she could keep or sell. She would make history as the youngest person ever to win the race—and a girl at that.

But Denny batted the thought from her mind as if it were a bothersome mosquito. She knew that only some teams would take the correct trail at the fork, lessening the chances of anyone else finding him. It could be hours before help arrived to pull them from the frigid water. Jasper and his remaining dogs had only minutes. If she left them, the river would swallow them up, purely and simply.

Remembering her grandfather's lessons, especially the story about the man who helped the little mouse, Denny stopped to help. She brought her team as close to the hole in the ice as she thought was safe and turned them around so that the dogs were facing away. Then she quickly tied a rope to the platform where she stood at the back, careful to secure it to the strongest part.

"Stay!" she shouted at Taz.

With her team in place, Denny crawled out toward Jasper with the other end of the rope in her hand. When she was as close as she dared be, she tossed the coiled end of the rope across the ice to Jasper, who managed to lay a soggy glove on the end, fumbling in his effort to grasp it. Shouting encouragement, Denny told him to tie the rope to his team.

"I can't," he said, his teeth chattering. "I can't move my fingers."

Denny slid closer to the edge of the hole, struggling to reach the rope's end. She heard the sound of the ice cracking beneath her a second before the shock of the cold water made her scream beneath the river's surface. When she emerged, she couldn't breathe and thought she was going to drown. When she finally managed a gasp and filled her lungs with air, she concentrated on trying not to panic. She pulled off her gloves using her teeth, found the end of the rope, and managed to tie a good, strong knot to the main line just where the lead dog was hooked. Then she turned toward her waiting team.

"Go!" she shouted, while she still could control her breathing.

Taz turned around and looked at her. Then he did as he had been taught. All eight members of Denny's team pulled and pulled against the dead weight. Little by little, dog by dog, they pulled Jasper's team from the water, but the two dead dogs and the dead weight of the sled were like an anchor catching on the lip of the ice, preventing further rescue. Denny saw that there was no way to save Jasper's team with the sled still attached. With the risk of everyone perishing, she pulled out her pocketknife and spoke to Jasper, who was barely able to keep his head above water.

"I have to cut the sled free or else we're all going to die."

Jasper nodded that he understood.

"Here, wrap your arm around the line here and hold on with all your strength," she said, helping him to hold the main line in the crook of his arm. "When I cut this, my dogs are going to pull you out. Don't let go."

With one hand firmly gripping the line, Denny sawed at the thick mainline with the other. Suddenly, her blade cut through.

"Taz! Go!" she shouted, choking on water. "Go!"

Free of the weight of the sled and with Jasper's team safely out of the water and on their feet, Denny and Jasper were pulled from the water. Taz and the other dogs kept pulling until they had dragged them clear of the river, up the bank and into the trees.

"Whoa! Whoa!" Denny shouted.

Although free of the icy water, Denny knew that they were still in danger of freezing to death.

"First things first," she said to Jasper, who was too cold and too exhausted to help. "I've got to tie off the teams so they don't run away and then build a fire to warm us up."

Denny always kept a butane lighter in a sealed plastic baggie, something she had learned from her grandfather. She remembered his exact words as they sat around a campfire. "The ability to make a fire in an emergency can sometimes be the difference between life and death. You must always be prepared for the worst."

While Jasper sat against the trunk of a tree shivering uncontrollably, Denny gathered up firewood, small pieces at first. She peeled off some small curly bark from a nearby birch tree and built a small pile of tinder. On top of the white, paper-thin birch bark, she gently piled thin pieces of dry limbs she broke off from underneath a scraggily spruce tree. With her hand shaking, she tried to ignite the lighter. The wind blew the flame away as soon as it appeared. She tried over and over, cupping a hand around the lighter to shield it from the wind. Finally, the wind died down for just a moment, and she was able to hold the yellow flame against the tender pile, which ignited quickly. For several minutes she knelt beside the small fire, feeding it larger and larger pieces of wood with her trembling hands, nurturing it as if it were a living thing.

Finally, the fire was roaring.

"It's going pretty good now," she proudly announced to Jasper.

But when she looked up, Jasper was unconscious with his head slumped on his chest. Denny's own breath stopped for a moment. She thought he was dead. She checked his breathing.

His pulse was faint, but he was still alive.

She had to work fast if she was going to save him. She tossed another handful of sticks on the growing fire and scrambled over to her sled. While Jasper's sled with all its survival gear lay at the bottom of the river, hers was safe and dry. She pulled out her sleeping bag, good to thirty below zero, and brought it close to the unconscious man. With difficulty, she removed his soaked high-tech parka and sweater, which were robbing his body of all its warmth. She also pulled off his wet boots and soggy socks and slipped on his feet a pair of her thick and itchy wool socks. With most of Jasper's wet clothes removed, Denny wrapped the sleeping bag around him as best she could, and then she got out of her own wet clothes.

She had to save herself if she was going to save anyone else.

With her dry clothes on, Denny helped the dogs, building several large fires near where they were tied up and heating water for their supper. She fed all twenty-two dogs a hot meal to warm their bellies and to give them energy to warm themselves from the inside out. While she worked, the storm died down. All the while, she kept an eye on the main fire, adding to it from time to time, and checking on the wet clothes hanging on sticks close to the fire to dry out. Her grandfather's red flannel shirt almost caught fire. When she felt the sleeping bag cloaked around Jasper's sleeping body, it was toasty hot.

Once the dogs were fed and settled, their fires stoked, Denny collapsed by the main fire to gather her strength. Jasper opened his eyes, looking around him, perplexed.

"You're safe," Denny said, adjusting the bag to better cover his neck.

"My dogs?" he croaked.

"They're alright, too. They're right over there warming up," replied Denny, deciding not to tell him that his sled and two of his dogs had been lost in the river.

Jasper nodded in appreciation and then closed his eyes and fell asleep again. A little later, when he came to, he asked, "How long was I out?"

Denny pulled up the cuff of her parka and looked at her wrist.

"I dunno. My watch is broke. The water must have ruined it. But it must have been at least a couple hours."

"It looks old," said Jasper, looking at the face of the watch.

"It was my grandfather's."

"I'm sorry. Can I see it?" he replied.

Denny thought from his tone that he must have heard about her grandfather, have some understanding of what the watch meant to her. She removed it and handed it to Jasper, who studied the face and the back.

"Maybe I can fix it," he said. "Band's in pretty bad shape, but I bet the guts can be repaired. Maybe just a good drying out. Can I borrow it?"

Denny nodded.

He tucked the watch into a pocket.

Denny told Jasper about his sled and his two dogs. The whole time Jasper just stared into the flames of the campfire. She knew how hard it would be if she had lost two of her dogs that way.

"How long were you in the water?" she asked.

"I don't rightly know. Too long," he replied slowly, without looking up from the mesmerizing flames.

About then, other teams began to arrive. One man gave Jasper a pair of dry long johns and dry pants. One shared his thermos of hot coffee.

"That'll warm up your insides," he said as Jasper took a sip. "You're lucky to be alive. Good thing the kid came along or you'd be a goner. You guys gonna scratch? You want me to contact the race officials and get some help?"

Denny looked at Jasper cradling the warm plastic cup of the thermos in his hands. He shook his head weakly.

Denny nodded that she understood.

"No," she said defiantly. "We're going to finish this race."

Seeing that the two mushers were okay, the other racers stayed only momentarily before they left, finding a safer place to cross downriver. Several took photographs of the hole in the ice. The finish line was close, less than thirty miles away, within easy reach.

It was hours before Denny and Jasper were ready to hit the trail. By then, every team still in the race had passed them. When she was ready, Denny tied Jasper's dogs to her team, with Taz in front to lead the way. With Jasper lying in the sleeping bag in the basket of the sled, still suffering from the effects of hypothermia, Denny drove the twenty-two-dog team—the largest in the race—along the edge of the frozen and windswept sea toward the finish line.

Looking up at the stars shivering between breaks in the clouds Denny couldn't help but be reminded of the terrible night her grandfather died.

The story of Denny's heroism and sacrifice beat her to the finish line, carried on the tongues and in the hearts of every racer who finished before her. By the time news arrived that she was only a few miles out of town, photographs of the accident were already making their way to newspapers and television stations. Some websites were already carrying the story. By morning, the whole world would know that 16-year-old Deneena Yazzie had her chance to win the race, but gave it up to save a fellow racer— Jasper Stark, no less, the three-time world champion.

It seemed as if every resident of the town lined both sides of the trail for the last half mile to the finish line. As Denny's team of twenty-two dogs passed through the cheering crowds, spectators waved handmade signs with her name, and children ran alongside the sled for as long as they could. Jasper waved feebly at the people from inside the sleeping bag in the sled's basket.

They had finished together, the very last team to cross the finish line. There would be no trophies, no new truck, and, most importantly, no prize money—no means by which Denny could support her team or get home. Although she smiled and waved at the people and the photographers, on the inside Denny was sad. She had come so far and worked so hard to be in the race. She had proved the worth of her team, almost winning, only to fail miserably.

Denny's disappointment was bitter in her throat.

As soon as her team came to a stop, medical doctors carefully helped Jasper from the basket and led him away to check his condition, and a race official awarded Denny a red hurricane lantern, a token traditionally bestowed on the last-place team as a symbol of a beacon of light to guide them safely home through the darkness. Like the Olympic torch, the little red lantern was lit when the race started, and it would only be extinguished after the last musher crossed the finish line, marking the end of the race.

Suddenly, Denny was smothered by reporters asking questions and by people congratulating her and shaking her hands. She couldn't figure out why they were congratulating her. She had lost. Much was made of the irony that Jasper Stark had predicted another win, even that he'd break his record, and yet he finished dead last. The reporters asked Denny what she was going to do next and if she was going to enter the race next year. Denny couldn't think that far ahead. Exhausted as she was, all she could think about as reporters shoved their microphones into her face was feeding her dogs and getting something to eat and going to bed.

"I don't know what I'm going to do," she replied in a haggard voice while rubbing her eyes. "I don't even know how I'm going to get home. I had hoped to win enough money to pay for a plane ticket and to buy food for my team for a year."

Finally, the crowd melted away like a late spring snow, going home or back to school or to work. After caring for the dogs, feeding them, and bedding them down for a long, deserved rest, and with no place else to go, Denny made her way to the Race Headquarters Office. Someone brought her a hot plate of pancakes covered with tinfoil, which she ate ravenously. While she ate, a nurse came in and told her that Jasper was going to be okay.

"Glad to hear it," Denny replied, putting down her cup of coffee. "Thanks for letting me know."

After breakfast, Denny sat on a chair beside the crackling barrel stove, took her diary out from her backpack, and wrote an entry, doodling in the margins.

Dear Nellie:

I didn't win the race. I had it, but then I lost it. I didn't win any of the prize money. Not a dime. I have no idea how I'm going to get home. But that doesn't worry me as much as what will happen to my team. Mother's going to sell off all the dogs. I worry most about Taz. What will happen to him? I'll have to let him go. But I guess with a spirit as free and wild as his, he never really was mine in the first place. I don't think I can face the people back home. Everyone's going to make fun of me saying stuff like, "There's that girl who thought she was better than everyone else!" Truth is I never thought I was better than anyone. I just don't believe that being a girl should keep me from following my dreams. All I ever wanted was to be connected to the land and to the old ways like Grandpa taught me. Everyone will think I couldn't have won anyway. They'll think I'm a loser because I was last. Grandpa would have understood, and he would have been proud of me. But I'm afraid no one else will.
Denny

18

K'edze' ghak'ae
Homecoming

The last thing Denny remembered was lying down on a cot that two volunteers had brought in for her. Several hours later, she was shaken awake.

"Are you Deneena Yazzie?" asked the bearded man leaning over her.

She struggled to wake up.

"Yeah," she answered groggily, hoping it was only a dream.

"I'm your pilot. It's time to go," said the man, looking down at her with his arms across his chest. "Your village airstrip is a pretty tough approach. I want to land before dark."

"Wha . . . what?" asked Denny, rubbing the sleep from her eyes and stretching out on the narrow cot. She had no idea how long she had been asleep.

"I'm supposed to take you home. Your team and your gear are already loaded. Time to get up, Sleepy Head. Let's go. Chop, chop. We're burning daylight."

As she was climbing into the plane, a red pickup drove up, the driver honking his horn and flashing his headlights. Jasper Stark stepped out from the passenger door and waved. Denny climbed back out from the cockpit.

"I wanted to catch you before you left," he yelled above the sound of the airplane engine. "I have something for you."

He handed Denny a small box with a card.

"What's this?"

"It's a gift."

Jasper leaned closer to speak above the engine noise.

"For saving my life. Go ahead, open it."

Denny opened the card, which read, "I'd be proud to share the trail with you any day."

Then she opened the box, which contained her grandfather's watch, only instead of the worn out leather band it had a brand-new gold band adorned with gold nuggets, quite expensive and quite fashionable by Alaskan standards.

"I thought you'd like that back. Hope you don't mind that I replaced the old band." Jasper smiled and winked. "I got it at a souvenir shop in town."

Denny saw that the second hand was moving.

"You fixed it!" she cried, and then she hugged Jasper.

"All it needed was a good drying out . . . like me."

From her seat beside the pilot, Denny looked out the windows as the small plane followed the frozen river. She saw herds of caribou on the hillsides and moose on the flats or among the patchwork of scraggly trees in the whiteness. Against the immense landscape, the small aircraft was little more than an invisible mote, a gnat, droning across the cloud-tangled sky. The pilot made occasional chit-chat with her.

There's so-and-so river or so-and-so lake, he'd say, pointing to some landmark below.

Finally, Denny got the nerve to say something she had been thinking about.

"I don't have any money to pay for this flight."

"Don't worry about it, kiddo. It's taken care of."

"You mean someone paid for it?" she asked incredulous. "Who?"

The pilot looked at Denny and smiled.

"Mr. Stark took care of the bill," he said.

Denny didn't say anything for a while after that. Although she was glad that the airplane debt was paid, she still worried about what would become of her team. Her mother had said she could keep the dogs only if she won enough money in the race to feed them. But Denny hadn't won a penny.

Now she would lose her team.

Worst of all, she would have to give up Tazlina.

Finally, Denny could see her village crouched along the northern shore. From above, the village looked tiny and misplaced in the vastness of the wilderness. The pilot banked the plane, turning toward the small airfield a mile out of town. After lining up the plane with the runway, he pushed in the throttle, checked his airspeed, trimmed the flaps, and spun a small, black wheel to change the angle of the nose as he began his approach to the airstrip. A few minutes later the craft landed, bouncing only once when the landing wheels touched down. Safely on earth, the pilot taxied toward the little parking area where Denny could see her mother's truck with a small trailer waiting to pick her up.

But after the prop stopped spinning and the pilot opened the door, Denny was surprised to see Silas step out from the driver's side.

"What are you doing here?" she asked, after climbing out the small door and ducking as she passed beneath the wing.

"Your mom asked me to come get you. She said she was too busy."

The news hurt. Denny thought for certain that her mother would come get her. She thought she might even be a little proud of her for finishing the race.

I guess it's hard to love a loser, she thought.

"Well," she said, shrugging her shoulders, "let's load up the dogs and my gear and go home."

Without saying a word, Denny transferred her team from the airplane to the back of the truck, one at a time, while Silas moved the bags of gear and loaded the sled onto the trailer, being careful to tie it down securely.

As Silas drove down the little road to the village, the empty plane took off, passing low above the truck, tipping its wings as it headed back to the city.

The village seemed asleep. No one was on the streets, except for a few roaming dogs that ran out and barked at the truck. Denny had imagined that some people might have shown a little interest in her adventure, at least asking how she did in the race.

"I need to stop here for a minute," said Silas as they were passing the community center where bingo and potlatches were held.

"Why?" asked Denny, looking at the empty parking lot.

"I need to do something," said Silas. "Why don't you come in with me?"

"I can't. I gotta put these dogs away and feed them. Besides, I'm pretty bushed. I haven't exactly got a lot of sleep lately."

"C'mon. It'll only take a minute," replied Silas, with a pleading smile, as he turned off the engine.

Grudgingly, Denny climbed out of the truck and slammed the squeaky door.

"This better not take too long," she said in a defeated tone.

Silas opened the outer door to the community hall for his friend.

"Age before beauty," he said, knowing that Denny was a few months older.

Denny stuck out her tongue.

"More like *age before ugly*," she said with a sly smirk, while opening the main door herself.

As soon as the door swung open, a loud chorus of shouts greeted her.

"S-U-R-P-R-I-S-E!"

It seemed as if everyone in the entire village was in the building. A large banner reading "Welcome Home Denny!" was strung across the room. Balloons were everywhere. When Denny stopped in her tracks, the hall burst into applause.

Several voices in the crowd shouted, "We love you, Denny!"

"Way to go!" a lone voice called out.

Silas stood beside her. He put a hand on the small of her back.

"This is all for you," he said, nudging her into the room.

With people still applauding, Denny crossed the plank floor and stood before a long table with three large cakes, each with one word written in frosting. Together, the three cakes spelled out, "Welcome Home Denny." Bowls of punch sat on either end of the table. A fourth, smaller cake, was shaped like a bone with the names of all eight dogs written on it.

Taz's name was the biggest.

Denny's mother and grandmother stepped out from the crowd and hugged her. Silas stepped back and watched, smiling and clapping. After the long embrace, Delia turned toward the audience and raised a hand. She spoke in a loud, practiced voice, used to addressing the community in the great hall.

The room slowly settled.

"I'd like to thank all of you for welcoming my daughter home," she said in a proud, strong voice.

Then she turned toward Denny.

"While you were gone, the whole village followed you on television, in the newspapers, and on the radio."

"And on the Internet!" some young person shouted.

"Yes, on that, too," Delia chuckled. "We watched you every day. All the kids at school made posters and maps to show where you were. We heard how you lost because you stopped to save another racer's life. We were all proud when the television reporter said that you had the biggest heart of anyone in the race. But we already knew that. Many reporters even came here to film our village to show the world where you come from. They pretty much talked to everyone."

The room filled with laughter.

"We're all proud of you," said Delia, her sweeping hand gesturing at all the smiling people in the large room. "I'm proud of you, too. And I know your grandfather would be very proud of you. *You* are his legacy. He lives inside *you*."

Denny's eyes welled up. She had to look down at the floor.

Her grandmother took her by the hand and gave it a reassuring squeeze. "You done good," she whispered into her granddaughter's ear. "Make you granddaddy proud."

"So," said Delia in a more upbeat tone, "let's get this party started!"

Everyone applauded again.

Delia raised her hands to settle the crowd once again.

"But before we cut these cakes, I'd like to thank a few people. First, I'd like to thank Denny's father who helped me to organize this party and pay for part of it."

Everyone looked around the room for Denny's father. It seemed as if everyone was whispering something to the person closest. Then Denny saw him. He was standing in the back of the hall by himself, leaning against the wall near the door with his arms across his chest.

When their eyes met, he smiled and bowed his head in acknowledgement.

Denny managed to smile back while wiping away tears.

"And the rest of the money?" said Delia. "The entire village donated the rest."

The room burst into applause yet again.

Once again Delia raised her hands above her head for quiet. When the applause died down she said, "I've saved the best for last. Just this morning our tribal office received an email for you.

I'd like to read it so everyone can hear."

Delia took out a folded piece of paper from her back pocket, cleared her voice once, and read the letter aloud.

Dear Ms. Deneena Yazzie:

The entire world watched in amazement at how you gave up the chance to win the world's greatest dogsled race to help an endangered fellow racer while others thought only of the finish line. Your brave and selfless actions were the embodiment of sportsmanship. We here at Husky Dog Foods would be proud to support you. On behalf of the Board of Directors, I am authorized to award you a one-year contract of sponsorship, which will pay for your dog team's food and veterinary care, the costs of entry fees, transportation, housing to participate in races, and a monthly stipend to cover other financial needs. We would be honored if you would wear our company logo on your outerwear.

Regards,

J. Roderick Clark, President

As they had done several times before, the entire community applauded. Some people in the audience whistled, and someone shouted, "You go, girl!"

Denny thought the voice sounded a lot like Silas'.

Delia gave the letter to her daughter and picked up a long kitchen knife from the table.

"Now, let's have some cake!" she declared.

As was done at potlatches, young people served, carrying slices of cake on flimsy, white paper plates to the elders. Most of the helpers were high school students. Even Mary Paniaq helped, even though Denny thought her belly looked so large that it might burst. Denny chuckled at the way Mary waddled about like a fat penguin.

Wherever she turned, Denny was shaking hands. The school teachers all hugged her. Valerie Charley grabbed her by the arm when she passed.

"I want to thank you," she said above the din of the celebration.

"For what?" asked Denny.

"For giving me the courage to follow my dreams. I told my boss I'm going to quit at the end of summer so I can go to college in the fall."

"Good for you! I know you can do it."

"*Tsin'aen*," replied a beaming Valerie, using the Indian word for thanks.

Denny saw her father still standing at the back of the room, close to the door, as if he needed to be near a way out. He looked as nervous as a caged wolf. She walked across the wide floor to bring him a piece of cake.

"I'm glad you're here," she said, handing him the small plate.

"Me too," replied her father.

Neither said a word for a couple minutes; they just stood side-by-side watching other people in the room, her father taking bites of the cake.

Denny broke the awkwardness.

"Thanks for helping Mom put on this party."

"No problem."

"That's not all he did," interrupted Delia, who had been standing nearby eavesdropping on their conversation. "Your father's the one who left the envelope on the door with enough money to pay for a hotel."

Denny was astonished.

"*You* did that?" she asked. "Where did you get the money? I'm sorry. That doesn't sound very thankful. I don't mean no disrespect."

"That's alright," he said, obviously uncomfortable. "I guess I got that coming. I raffled one of my potlatch rifles during Bingo Night."

"But . . . how did you guys know I needed money?" Denny asked.

Delia looked down at the floor.

"I . . . I read your dairy," she replied sheepishly. "You left it on your bed one day."

Denny's face showed her terror.

"How . . . how much did you read?"

"All of it," replied her mother, sheepishly. "I'm sorry. I was worried about you."

Denny was concerned about some of the things her mother must have read in the pages. In her mind, she thought about certain passages, especially the critical ones about her mother. But her mother gently took her face in both hands and looked deep into her heart through the blue wells of her eyes.

"You're wrong about one thing," she said tenderly. "You're my daughter. I love you with all my heart."

With her whole body atremble, Denny hugged her mother as tight as she could with her face buried in her mother's shoulder to hide her tears and to muffle her sobbing.

"I'm sorry," she said over and over.

Her father stood beside them, uncertain what to do, unused to displays of affection.

Looking up from the embrace, Denny saw Mary Paniaq turn and run outside. Worried that she was having a miscarriage, Denny ran after her. Mary was leaning against the outside of the building, her whole body shaking.

"Are you alright?" Denny asked, putting a hand on Mary's shoulder.

"No one loves me like that. No one cares about me."

Denny turned Mary around so that they were facing each other.

"That's not true and you know it," she said sternly.

Mary sniveled before she spoke.

"Name one person who cares about me. Just one."

"I do, Mary. I care about you."

Mary broke out into even more tears and sobbing.

"Why? Why do you care so much?"

"Because you're part of this community," replied Deneena. "We're a family. We have to help each other. I want to help you."

Mary wiped her face with the back of her hand.

"I don't know what to do. I'm so afraid. I got this kid inside me. I gotta raise her by myself. My whole life is ruined."

"It's okay to be afraid. We're all afraid sometimes. But you're not alone and your life isn't ruined. Do you hear me? It's not ruined. But you have to stop drinking and doing all that other crap or else you could ruin your baby's life."

"I'll . . . I'll try," said Mary.

"No. That's not good enough. You have to stop right now," Denny said sternly. "I'll help you. Promise me. Promise you'll stop."

"You'll help me?" Mary sniveled again.

Denny smiled.

"Whatever it takes. You know I'm good for my word."

"I promise," said Mary, looking down and caressing her taut belly.

The two teenage girls held each other with their hearts pressed close together—the weaker gaining strength and courage from the stronger. Eventually, they went back inside where it was warm.

Later, after almost everyone had left, Silas walked up to Denny with both hands in his pockets.

"Pretty good party, huh?"

"It was wonderful."

"Bet you didn't expect it."

"Nope. Bet you didn't expect *this*," Denny said, as she punched Silas on the shoulder and giggled.

"Ouch!" said Silas, rubbing his shoulder. "You're strong . . . for a girl."

Denny reached into her pants pocket and pulled out a small, smooth stone and handed it to her friend.

"What's this?" he asked.

"I don't need it anymore," replied Denny. "I know who I am and where I come from."

While her mother and grandmother stayed behind to help clean up the community center hall, Denny drove home to unload the dogs and feed them their supper, giving each one an extra piece of dried salmon and a well-deserved pat on the head. When they were done eating, Denny gave each dog a slice of the bone-shaped cake.

Taz got the one with his name written in blue frosting.

Afterward, though dead tired, Denny drove up to the cemetery on the hill overlooking the village and stood beside the white-washed picket fence with the waist-high, brightly painted house enclosed, a temporary home for the spirit.

"I did it, Grandpa. I finished the race just like I promised," she said.

A raven alighted on a nearby cross and ruffled his wings before hunkering down against the cold.

"I wish you could have seen me. You would have been proud," she said, tearfully. "I remembered the things you taught me, like the story about the mouse and about not putting myself above others. I think things are going to be better between me and my dad. I think he's proud of me, even though he can't say it yet."

The raven cawed.

"I miss you."

The raven cawed again.

Denny placed the red lantern on her grandfather's grave and wiped her eyes.

"This is to help you find your way home," she said so softly that a breeze swept her words over the hill and across the quiet river.

The raven flew away.

A little later, back home as the sun began to set, Denny untied Tazlina, and together—a girl and a wolf—they wandered down to the river, sat side-by-side on the bank, and gazed at the snowy mountains turning pink in the twilight. They listened to the swaying and creaking trees and marveled at a playful raven reeling and tumbling on a crosswind, until the thin, dark-blue pencil stroke of dusk finally turned to night.

References

Glossary of Indian Words
by Chapter

All words in Ahtna (pronounced ot-naw), an endangered Athabaskan language from Alaska's vast interior, come from the author's *Ahtna Noun Dictionary and Pronunciation Guide* (1998, 1999, 2011; foreword by Noam Chomsky and Steven Pinker). Mentored by the legendary M.I.T. linguist, Ken Hale, John Smelcer is also the editor-compiler of the *Alutiiq Noun Dictionary and Pronunciation Guide* (2011, foreword by the Dalai Lama and Eyak Chief Marie Smith). Both dictionaries can be accessed at www.johnsmelcer.com (click on Dictionaries). In the spring of 2011, the author gave a lecture on his linguistic work at Harvard University's Lamont Library as part of their Omniglot Seminars. All myths come from the author's *In the Shadows of Mountains* (1997) and *The Raven and the Totem* (1992). All bilingual poems come from the author's *Beautiful Words: The Complete Ahtna Poems* (2011), a landmark in American literature and American Indian Studies. The helpful pronunciation guide below uses rudimentary English phonetics. Note: The slashed-L (Ł or ł) sound is generally unpronounceable to non-Native speakers.

Song of the Wind

(Word)	(Definition)	(Pronunciation
Łts'ii c'eliis	Wind Song	[chee kay-lees]
ts'abaeli	spruce tree	[chaw-bell-lee]
ghelaay	mountain	[ga-lie-ee]
K'ełt'aeni	Mt. Sanford	[kelth-taw-nee]
saghani	raven	[saw-gaw-nee]
Saghani Ggaay	the mythic figure,	[saw-gaw-nee guy]
	Raven, the Trickster	
udzih taas	caribou soup	[you-jee toss]
ts'inst'e'e	old woman	[chin-steh]
da'atnae	old man	[daw-ot-na]
tsa hwnax	outhouse	[chaw nock]

Note: *Tsa* means "poop/feces." The word for grizzly bear is *tsaani* (literally "bear that smells like poop"). Thus, *tsa hwnax* literally means "poop house."

sezel	steam bath, sweathouse	[sez-el]

Note: The word for Saturday is *sezel ggaay* ("little steam bath"); the word for Sunday is *sezelce'e* ("big steam bath").

Land of Ice

nen' tae dlii	land of ice	[nen ta dlee]
dligi	squirrel	[dlee-gee]
tikaani	wolf	[tik-aw-nee]
tsa'	beaver	[chaw]
tsa' zes	beaver pelt/skin	[chaw zess]

To learn more about the fatal wolf attack on a rural Alaskan teacher in March 2010, go to www.msnbc.msn.com/id/35913715/us_news_life, or go to http://articles.latimes.com/2010/mar/13/nation/la-na-wolf-attack13-2010mar13, or simply Google the keywords <wolf attack Alaska teacher 2010>. Alaska Native Billie (neé Carter) Upland's mother was killed by wolves at Ft. Yukon in the 1950s while walking home from the village general store with a bag of groceries. The author of this novel survived a wolf attack just outside the northern boundary of Denali National Park.

River's Edge

na' baaghe	river's edge	[naw baw-way]
deniigi	moose	[deh-nee-gee]
ggax	rabbit	[gok; also gak]

(Note: a local river is called Gakona [gaw-koe-na], literally "Rabbit River")

dluuni	mouse	[dloo-nee]
tsin'aen	thank you	[chin-nen]

The bilingual poem "On Feet of Clouds" is on permanent display at the red wolf exhibit of Chicago's Brookfield Zoo.

Spirit of the Trail

ceyiige' gha tene	spirit of the trail	[kay-yee-geh wa ten-eh]
guuxi	coffee	[goo-kee; English loanword]
utniil	oatmeal	[oot-neel; English loanword]
stakalbaey	camprobber	[stock-all-bay]
cen'łkatl'i	woodpecker	[ken-skaw-klee]

Note: *cen* is a root word that refers to wood/plants; e.g. stick, root, trunk, stalk

yanida'a	mythic times	[yan-ee-daw-ah]
ciił	young man	[keeth]
nel'ii	black bear	[nell-ee]

Words Have Teeth

hnae ghu' 'aen	words have teeth	[na woo an]
xał	sled	[hoth]
xał tl'aaxi	sled runners	[hoth tlaw-kee]
xał yii	sled basket	[hoth yee]
xał dzaade'	brace, stanchion	[hoth jaw-deh]
xał daten'	sled handle	[hoth daw-ten]
łitl'uule'	main line	[thlit-loo-leh]
ciz'aani	heart	[kiz-zaw-nee]

Note: The bilingual poem "Heart" can be heard read aloud by the author at *Harvard Review Online*.

A Day's Journey

ts'iłk'ey dzaen yuuł	one day journey	[chell-kay jan yoolth]
xonahang	goodbye	[hoe-naw-hong]
'aat'	wife	[s-aht; pron. as two syllables]
ts'anyae	burbot	[chen-ya]
tsaey	tea	[chie; Russian loanword]

Potlatch

hwtiitł	potlatch	[koo-teeth; also who-teeth]
dzoogaey	potlatch guests	[joo-gay]

hwtiitł ts'ede'	potlatch blanket	[who-teeth ched-eh]
tsa'	beaver	[chaw]
nuuni	porcupine	[noo-nee]
deyaazi	cow moose	[day-yaw-zee]
hwtiitł kołdogh	potlatch speech	[koo-teeth kolth-doe]
Tsisyu	Paint Clan	[shish-you]

Note: the author is a member of Tsisyu Clan; his father is Talcheena Clan

Talcheena	comes from the sea	[tal-chee-naw]
ghleli	drum	[lay-lee] also [way-lee]
hwtiitł c'edzes	potlatch dance	[koo-teeth ked-zess]

Note: In his lifetime, John Smelcer has participated in dozens of potlatches across Alaska, including the potlatches for Chief Harry Johns of Copper Center and Chief Walter Northway of Northway Village, who, it is said, was 117 years old when he died. John has been part of the hosting family on numerous occasions, such as on the death of his great aunt and great uncle, Joe and Morrie Secondchief, and the deaths of his beloved uncle and grandmother, Herbert Smelcer and Mary Joe Smelcer (photos of the potlatch for John's grandmother can be seen on the author's website; click on bio or photo gallery). In the spring of 1978, while in junior high school, John participated in the "Stick Dance," an annual potlatch held in Nulato, an Eskimo village on the lower Yukon River. The trip was sponsored by the Johnson O'Malley Program for Native students. In 1996, John received a grant from the State of Alaska to hold a series of workshops in Copper Center so that he and elders could teach Indian youth how to sing, dance, and drum for the potlatch. John's great grandfather, Tazlina Joe, was instrumental in taking the potlatch underground during its prohibition from the late 1800s until about the 1940s.

January

'Aîts'eni na'aaye'   Fifth Month   [alt-say-nee naw-eye]

Note: Winters in interior Alaska are so cold and so long that seven of the winter months are simply numbered. January is the "fifth month of snow." Let's learn to count to ten in Ahtna: (1) *ts'eîk'ey* [chell-kay], (2) *nadaeggi* [na-da-gee], (3) *taa'i* [taw-kee], (4) *denc'ih* [denk-ee], (5) *aîts'eni* [alt-say-nee], (6) *gistaani* [gist-aw-nee], (7) *konts'aghi* [kont-sa-gee], (8) *îl'edenc'ih* [ka-denk-ee], (9) *ts'eîk'ey kole* [chell-kay kwal-aye], (10) *hwlazaan* [la-zon].

Swift River

Tezdlen Na'   Tazlina River   [tez-dlen-naw]

Note: The word literally means "swift river." Nowadays, the river is conveniently spelled *Tazlina* [taz-lee-na]. Since the early 1990s, the author's little rustic cabin has perched on the bluff above the confluence of the Copper and Tazlina Rivers overlooking the family fish-wheel and the snowy Wrangell Mountains where his ancestor's spirits are said to dwell.

February

Gistaani na'aaye'   Sixth Month   [gis-taw-nee naw-eye]

The Girl with the Black Wolf

t'aede kae tikaani t'uuts'   "teenage girl with black wolf"
                                    [ta-deh ka tik-aw-nee toots-sen]

Note: An adult woman is called *ts'akae* [chass-ka]

ciz'aani	heart	[kiz-zaw-nee]

On the Face of Things

uyida' neltats'	chin tattoo	[oo-yee-da nell-tats]

Note: The Ahtna word for chin is *uyida'*.

City of Ants

nadosi	ant, ants	[na-doe-see]
nadosi tene	ant road	[na-doe-see ten-eh]
nadosi kayax ce'e	big village of ants	[na-doe-see kie-yok kek-eh]

Note: *kayax* means village; *ce'e* means big or large

kon' tuu	whiskey, liquor	[kon-too]

Note: *kon' tuu* means "firewater," because liquor burns the mouth and throat.

Denny's Journey Begins

yuuł tezyaa	journey starts	[yooth tez-yaw]

High Country

ghelaay nen'	mountain country	[ga-lie-ee nen]

A Rising Star

son'de'aa	star rises; goes up	[son deh-daw]

Lone Wolves

The Storm Passes

hw'eł kuzyaa   (snow)storm passes   [who-eth kooz-yaw]

Homecoming

k'edze' ghak'ae   returning home   [kej-eh wa-ka]

Glossary of Mushing Terms

Basket	The "belly" of the sled in which cargo is transported, including gear, a person, or a sick dog
Booties	A kind of doggie boot fastened with Velcro, worn to protect paws (thrown booties are frequently found on the trail)
Brake	A hinged metal device mounted at the back of the sled that the musher can depress by foot to slow or stop the sled
Come Gee!	Command to turn completely around right
Come Haw!	Command to turn completely around left
Dog in Basket	Referring to an exhausted or injured dog riding in the basket of the sled

Double Lead — Two lead dogs at the front (usually on parallel tow lines)

Dropped Dog — A dog that has been "scratched" from the team or race, usually because of poor health or exhaustion

Gee — Command to go right (pronounce the hard "g" as in "gate")

Haw — Command to go left

Indian Dog — Any sled dog from a Native village

Lead Dog/Leader — The dog at the front of team, usually the smartest and fastest

Line Out! — Command to lead dog to pull the team straight from the sled (to help ease hooking and unhooking of the team)

Mush! — Command to lead dog to start the team. This command varies. Some mushers say Go! or Let's Go!; some say All Right! Any start command may be used

Neck Line — A short rope that connects a dog's collar to the tow line

Overflow — Water from rivers or creeks, lakes or ponds, that rises above the ice and flows—concealed—beneath the snow. Getting wet at below-zero temperatures can be dangerous, even life-threatening

Pedaling	Pushing the sled with one foot while keeping the other on the runner
Rigging	A general term for all the lines used to attach dogs to the sled
Runners	The two long bottom pieces of a sled, which come into contact with the snow. Modern mushers affix Teflon strips to the runners, which are replaced often
Scratch	To remove or disqualify a dog or a team from a race for a variety of reasons, often for poor health
Snow Hook	A metal device attached to the sled with a short rope and embedded in packed snow to keep the sled from moving
Snub Line	A rope used to secure the sled to a tree or other immovable object
Stake	A wooden or metal post (like a long tent stake) driven into the snow to which an individual dog or the tether line is attached
Swing Dogs	The dog(s) directly behind the lead dog that help turn the team
Tether Line	A long chain or rope with shorter chains or ropes extending from it at intervals, used when trees or stakes aren't available

Tow Line	Also called the main line, which connects dogs to the sled
Trail!	Yelled between mushers to request right-of-way on the trail
Tug Line	A short line that connects the dog's harness to the tow line
Wheel Dog(s)	The dog(s) closest to the sled, whose job is to pull the sled around tight corners or trees
Whoa!	Command to stop the team. Some mushers simply shout "Stop!"

Discussion Questions for
Lone Wolves

1. Denny does not believe that she is brave because she is scared. What does it mean to be brave? When does Denny show her bravery the most?

2. Denny is the only young person in the village who wants to learn the old ways of her people, including learning to speak their dying language. Why is preservation of culture so important? As a class, share your own family's heritage and traditions.

3. Silas and Denny discuss peer pressure. Who do you think is right, Silas or Denny? Have you ever felt pressured to do things you normally wouldn't do?

4. Alexie Senungutuk is a bully who demoralizes Denny. Have you or someone you know been bullied at school? Have you bullied others? What can you do to stop bullies?

5. Denny's grandfather teaches her about respecting nature. After his death, Denny vows to live like him. What do you think of Denny's choice?

6. Mary and the other teenagers don't seem to care about their lives; their only concern is to get away from the village. Why do you think someone would feel like that? What would happen to a small, tight-knit community if all the young people moved away? What could they do to change their lives for the better?

7. Taz is connected to Denny because they are both different, they are both *outcasts*. How do our differences make us special?

8. Many of the villagers want to go to the city to live better lives, but when they get there many end up disillusioned. What does this say about people always wanting more? Is the grass really greener?

9. How does the relationship between Denny and her mother change throughout the story?

10. Denny's father pretends that Denny does not exist. Denny's grandfather tells her it is because he is angry at the world and ashamed of himself. Is the way he treats his daughter any different than the way he is treated by other villagers? How do you think the relationship between Denny and her father changes at the end?

11. As a project, choose a musher in the Iditarod (The Great Race) and follow his or her progress throughout the race,

mapping out his 1,100 mile journey. Write a blog about your racer (where he comes from, if he's raced before, the names of all his dogs, etc.) and include facts about the race, dog sledding, and the rugged Alaskan wilderness.

The Author

John Smelcer is the poetry editor of *Rosebud* magazine and the author of more than forty books. He is an Alaskan Native of the Ahtna tribe, and is now the last tribal member who reads and writes in Ahtna. John holds degrees in anthropology and archaeology, linguistics, literature, and education. He also holds a PhD in English and creative writing from Binghamton University, and formerly chaired the Alaska Native Studies program at the University of Alaska Anchorage.

His first novel, *The Trap*, was an American Library Association BBYA Top Ten Pick, a VOYA Top Shelf Selection, and a New York Public Library Notable Book. *The Great Death* was short-listed for the 2011 William Allen White Award, and nominated for the National Book Award, the BookTrust Prize (England), and the American Library Association's Award for American Indian YA Literature. His Alaska Native mythology books include *The Raven and the Totem* (introduced by Joseph Campbell). His short stories, poems, essays, and interviews have appeared in hundreds of magazines, and he is winner of the 2004 Milt Kessler Poetry Book Award and of the 2004 Western Writers of America Award for Poetry for his collection *Without Reservation*, which was nominated for a Pulitzer. John divides his time between a cabin in Talkeetna, the climbing capitol of Alaska, where he wrote much of *Lone Wolves*, and Kirksville, Missouri. For more information, go to www.johnsmelcer.com.

The Illustrator

Hannah Carlon, 17, is a Cape Cod high school student and artist who studied under Eiblis Cazeault, Sarah Holl, and Carl Lopes.

About the Type

This book was set in Adobe Caslon, a typeface originally released by William Caslon in 1722. His types became popular throughout Europe and the American colonies, and printer Benjamin Franklin used hardly any other typeface. The first printings of the American Declaration of Independence and the Constitution were set in Caslon. For her Caslon revival for Adobe, designer Carol Twombly studied specimen pages printed by William Caslon between 1734 and 1770.

Designed by John Taylor-Convery
Composed at JTC Imagineering, Santa Maria,CA